Fry the Little Fishes

Also by Matt McGinn
  Scottish Songs of Today
  published by Harmony Music
  Once Again Matt McGinn
  published by Heathside Music

Matt McGinn has written over a thousand songs
of which a hundred and thirty are on record

Fry the Little Fishes

by

Matt McGinn

Calder & Boyars
London

First published in Great Britain 1975
by Calder & Boyars Ltd
18 Brewer Street London W1R 4AS

© Matt McGinn

2998

ISBN 0 7145 0992 2 Case bound Edition

Typeset in Great Britain by
Specialised Offset Services Limited, Liverpool
and printed by Whitstable Litho, Kent.

Fry the Little Fishes

CHAPTER 1

On awakening, Brother Gabriel tightened his buttocks and stretched his long, muscular legs till the toes reached the foot-spar of his narrow iron bed. He placed his hands between his legs as though wishing to choke what he found there, but resisted the temptation as Brother Gabriel had always resisted temptation.

His eyes, colourless in the inky blackness of the night, were now wide and blinklessly open as he allowed himself a moment's stoical elation, contemplating with pleasure and pride the fact that of all the Brothers in Saint Martin's he was the only one with his own inbuilt alarm system, and that on this cold winter morning, as on every other morning in his years in Saint Martin's he had again awakened unaided by either mortal or mechanical assistance.

Believing that idleness was evil and that vigorous physical activity was the answer to all the ills and sins of mankind, his code was a strict one, and he lived rigidly by its rules, scorning from the very start the services of Feeney, the night-watchman, for the very first act of the day — the opening of the eyes — at four forty-five.

Now it was on the hour and he lay listening as Feeney knocked on the doors of all the others including Brother Leon whose door lay directly across the corridor from Gabriel's. Leon: a smile crossed his face stretching his thick-lipped mouth to twice its normal length as he thought of what little Brother Leon would not give for his, Gabriel's, own clockwork brain which obeyed, first thing in the morning, his last command of an evening. 'Wake me at five to five.'

Leon, being a heavy sleeper, had suffered many embarrassments in the morning, often arriving late for meditation, unshaven and with collar askew, until he had been forced to purchase a little alarm clock with large luminous hands to aid him in what he considered to be the most demanding of tasks.

Not so Gabriel! His awakening was the result of his own unfailing will-power and he was proud of it, as indeed Brother Gabriel was proud of everything he did.

Now, as he heard Feeney's footsteps fade down the corridor, he quickly and vigorously jumped from the bed, took the one step necessary to reach the already open window, gave a smart tug at the cord of the heavy black-out blind, expanded his lung muscles and inhaled deeply the morning air.

Outside, all was quiet, dark and still.

Before the war he had enjoyed the early morning view from this window. Beyond and below the grounds of Saint Martin's he had seen the unsleeping lights of the still sleeping city and this sight had never failed to give him a sense of power and superiority.

But now all of Glasgow was black, lightless and in mourning. Even on fine summer mornings, the only sign Gabriel had of where the fields and trees of Saint Martin's ended and where Glasgow began was the black smoke-cloud which was a permanent umbrella to the city.

However, the darkness itself wasn't a bad thing. He recalled the morning some months back, when raising the blind, he had been momentarily stunned by what at first sight, appeared to be the whole city in flames. As it turned out, it had been only part of the outskirts of the great conurbation. Was it Clydebank? Brother Gabriel

2

could not at that moment recall the details, but had the impression that it had somehow been connected with the shipyards. He remembered that one of the boys had been given compassionate leave as he had lost some relation or other on that particular night. However, God's will be done . . . enough of these melancholy thoughts. He, Brother Gabriel had his own job to do and although this had become increasingly difficult as a result of the war and the blackout, when more and more youngsters were getting into trouble, causing enormous staffing and accommodation problems, his first duty must be to Saint Martin's; yes, Saint Martin's must come first. He must dismiss from his mind disturbing thoughts of the outside world which might depress him on this fine, crisp morning.

Having already lost precious minutes, he moved towards the wash-basin and with a swift, almost angry jerk, pulled off his night-shirt and, in the image of God and man, began to scrub and rinse every inch and crevice of his fine, strong body, which, in weaker moments, he had been heard — almost sacriligously — to boast, was the result of his early practice of Gaelic football and his good Flanagan stock.

Moving quickly, fixing his split-bibbed Marist collar over his long black robe, Gabriel was ready and listening for the opening of Brother John's door.

Something which never failed to amuse the other brothers was the fact that poor John suffered from some kind of a sleeping sickness which made him nod off at the oddest moments in the oddest places, and unfailingly in the chapel during morning meditation. For many years now his custom, strongly approved of by the others, had been to select a spot some distance from them on the very last pew where he would snooze and sometimes even snore, giving rise to remarks that he was merely leaving one bed for another.

Witticisms, notwithstanding, it had become their habit that Brother John should lead the small band from the north wing and no-one dared leave their room until they heard John's door open and close. Then in silent formation behind him, the black and white figures would wind their way, hands reverently clasped and eyes firmly fixed on the bare stone floors, along the dimly lit, white-tiled corridors, which to the uninitiated as indeed to the initiated, appeared almost foreboding.

This morning was no exception; as door after door opened and closed, including Leon's – who today appeared as crisp and fresh as Gabriel himself – Gabriel took up his position behind the others and silently joined the procession which would wend its way past the kitchens, the classrooms and the boys' dormitories, to the end of the corridor and finally arrive at the small chapel, for this hour of meditation at the start of a new day.

As the minute hand of the big, utilitarian clock moved to make a straight line with its partner on the hour, Feeney, poised and waiting beneath it, again blessed the the luck which had seventeen years before brought him to Saint Martin's. Of course 'luck' wasn't exactly the word to describe it. God and Father McGuinness, now long since gone, had really been responsible. But if he hadn't been such a devout man in the first place, he would never have been given this position at the approved school. Why, wasn't it he, Tom Feeney, who had planned and practically single handed,

4

dug and planted the gardens of the new Saint Simon's
Chapel almost nineteen years before? Two summers it
had taken him and little he had asked in return, but God
had rewarded him. HE had come to his aid in the guise
of the old Father McGuinness who had found him this
situation at Saint Martin's.

It didn't pay much then, only two pounds a week,
and the odd food parcel from the kitchen; of course
night-work didn't suit every man, but not having a wife,
Tom didn't mind; and for one who had had to leave
school at fourteen, he felt that he had indeed made the
best of himself and had responsibility normally awarded
to few with his background. Responsibility, Tom felt,
suited him. Where else would a man like himself, in his
own way, be responsible for a hundred and fifty boys?
Yes, like now. One clap of his hands on the hour of six
and this would signal to one hundred and fifty boys that
a new day had begun. That they, on hearing Tom
Feeney clap his hands together, in a way that was now a
practised and efficient movement, must rise, dress, and
set about their allotted work for the day pleased Tom.

Now the minute hand was at twelve, Feeney was, as
always, ready. CLAP! Yes, he was in good form this
morning. He lost no time now. Moving from door to
door up the corridor, at each door he repeated the
action. Hands apart to come together in each dramatic
– CLAP – and again at the next door – CLAP! With
each repetition of the movement Feeney could feel the
sublimity of it. Here, with his own hands, he could bring
to life one hundred and fifty human beings and send
them scurrying like ants hither and thither in a thousand
directions.

It was a power he could never get used to and of
which he could never have too much.

5

Each thunderous smack of flesh upon flesh had its own magical effect and Feeney viewed with satisfaction the sight of boys and young men, some of them designated as the toughest that Glasgow's slums could produce, as they tumbled obediently from bed, stumbled half-asleep to toilets, returned to pull off night-shirts, and don trousers, shirts and slippers; then without losing a moment, they would push beds to one side of their dormitories, take sweeping-brushes, floor cloths and dusters and long-handled floor polishers and bees-wax polish, and just as quickly and smartly set about their business chores like the inhabitants of a hive.

Yes, Tom had trained them well and he was proud!

But the allocation of dormitory chores was very much a matter for the boys themselves, the job of each indicating the pecking order, and inevitably to the toughest in physique or personality went the most prestigious chore.

Dormitory Two was no exception and Lammy Goodall had always been in charge of the polisher. His task it was to throw down the bees-wax for lowly folk like Patchy Kelly to rub into the stained wooden floor, and on completion of this menial task, he Lammy, would then attack the waxed wooden floorboards with strong, proud, sideward movements of the heavy polisher.

'Right down on your knees, ya patchy-heided bastard!' roared Lammy, giving the other boy a push to emphasize the words.

Patchy dropped to the floor, wincing as his bare knees came into contact with the wood. Tears rose to his eyes as he picked up his piece of duster and with two hands clasped about it, pushed forward, then back, rubbing the bees-wax hard into the already shining boards.

Big Noddy, he had started it, thought the boy. Yes, Big Noddy, who had been the 'donner' of Saint Martin's and Supervisor Curran . . . Supervisor Curran of the Saint Vincent Street Remand Home . . . they were the ones.

Twenty-three boys, Supervisor Curran had had in his charge and to break the monotony for them and for himself, he had been taking them from the dingy dismal 'Games Room' into the dark and equally dismal 'Projector Room' for a silent film show.

As the boys shuffled in single file from one well-barred room to another, Supervisor Curran stood where he was best able to view all the boys. As they passed his towering figure, he laid a heavy hand on the head of each . . . four . . . five . . . six . . . the little bits of scruff. God! he thought, What kind of homes did they come from? Filthy, mucky, some of them were when they came in here . . . and this new lot looked a right clatty bunch . . . nine . . . ten . . . all except that one with the sports jacket – comes from Giffnock too . . . imagine somebody in here from a lovely area like Giffnock . . . well seen he's a poof . . . not sixteen yet, and he's a poof . . . thirteen . . . fourteen . . . caught with some dirty midden in Saint Enoch's. But look at that lassie down the stairs, same age and she's on the 'game' . . . imagine . . . terrible . . . 'though I widnae mind masel' . . . nineteen . . . Christ, you do see life here.

Curran's thoughts were interrupted as his hand now rested on the head of Thomas B. Kelly.

'Here, whit's this, eh?'
'It's a boil sir.'
'A boil?'

'Aye.'

'Stand you to the side . . . twenty-two . . . twenty-three . . ."

'Now don't make any noise in there', he roared at the assembled boys. 'Right you,' and he pushed Patchy into a chair, at the same time producing his clipper. It cannot be denied that there are times and places where a scalped head can be a mark of honour, but Patchy was neither a Buddhist priest nor a cadet in the Russian Military Academy, and the judge before whom he was to make his appearance the following day might well look upon the baldy head as being a scabby one. He didn't doubt someone would condemn him, concluding that this scabby-head, baldy boy could only have come from a scabby-headed, unclean home. He might then decide that the person before him would be much better off in a clean, spartan institution such as Saint Martin's – of which he had heard nothing but glowing reports, presented biennially and triennially by perfectly reliable, middle-class inspectors.

So it was scarcely the most opportune moment for Patchy to have a 'baldy', but the possible effect of it on the judge was far removed from his mind as in the topmost and loneliest dormitory in the Remand Home, he cried and prayed and cooried himself to sleep.

Two days later Thomas B. Kelly, head scalped to the bone, exposing for all to see the two burn marks at the back, had entered Saint Martin's Approved School for Boys.

Saint Martin's was a planet of its own.

It might be affected by such things as air raids which would send the boys scampering (if scampering can be done in a disciplined manner) to the cellars, or by a certain deterioration in the food, an inevitability of war;

8

but otherwise it had little contact with and was little affected by the outside world.

It had its own farm and garden, its own shoemaking, joinery and tailoring shops and its own laundry. It was so self-sufficient that the postman did not have to call; the mail was collected by the most privileged boy in the school – the 'office boy' – who made daily trips to the town on various errands; he was much envied by the others for his dapper short-trousered suit. There were visitors once a month and when you had been there seven months, you were allowed home on a Sunday – after Mass and a sausage roll breakfast – until four-thirty in the afternoon. Ten days were allowed at Christmas, Easter and during the summer, when the boys could leave its confines for the outside world only to return more disgruntled and restless than before.

Immediately on entering Saint Martin's, Patchy had been ushered into the Prefect's Room. There he exchanged the neat little suit his mother bad bought, (to make him look tidy in front of the Sheriff in Brunswick Street) for his 'all day clothes', which could best be described as well-darned rags which seemed to have been successfully designed to humiliate. As Patchy neatly folded his new trousers and jacket and wondered if they would fit him when he got out; he thought of the last new suit that he had had.

Little velvet trousers and jacket, blouse, tie, top hose and shoes; even his underwear had been new. How happy he had been! 'Napoleon,' the teacher had said, 'When he was in exile was asked "Of all your victorious days, which was the happiest?" and he replied, "The day I made my first Holy Communion."

And so it was with Thomas B. Kelly, as he had donned his little velvet suit and satin blouse and

9

remembered the ecstacy of Confession. Followed by the purifying experience of Communion, he had felt a saintliness and a kinship with God – and even Napoleon. He knew that the wafer of unleavened bread, which was different from any bread he had ever tasted, was not really bread, but the Body of Christ. It was dry on his palate, but had melted and he would not have touched it with his teeth as this would have been 'like digging nails into the body of Christ,' Miss Tolland had said.

The feeling of spirituality remained with him as the procession of little girls in virgin-white dresses and veils and boys in neat little suits – the less reverent giggling and smiling at fawning parents, the more pious like Patchy, with hands clasped before them and eyes open only enough to allow them to see where they were going – made their way to the Chapel hall for the tea-breakfast which had been donated by the local bookie.

The happy recipient of a brand new penny, the boy and his proud parents then made their way to Jerome's in the Trongate where the great event was recorded for ever in the form of a photograph.

His da' who had worked like the devil for weeks before Tommy's Communion, touring the town with his basket of bananas so that he could pay-up for the velvet suit and the satin blouse, had given his son a threepenny piece when the boy had told him that it had been the happiest day he had ever had.

Tommy's life had continued on a fairly even keel for the next few years. 'A bright boy,' his mother had been told when he refused to attend the Academy and had opted for the Junior Secondary where his pals were. What good were French and Latin to him? he thought. When he was grown up he would be a hawker like his da', and if he worked hard enough he could maybe even get a stall at the barrows and be rich like Bobby Thomson in the pawn close who had a smashing house and a radiogram and a van. French and Latin, they were for the 'toffs' who were going to be teachers or priests and when had a teacher or priest ever come from Dalmarnock?

A few years later his da' collapsed and died while selling his bananas and it seemed to the boy as he stood in Saint Martin's in his darned jersey and short trousers that life had been one long unhappy tale since that day – and that tale had culminated in his entry to the Approved School.

A new boy was inferior to every other. By the general run of things, every one of those others would be 'out for good' before him, and being 'out for good' was what every one in the place desired more than anything else. When you were 'new' you were by a certain unbreakable law, the lowest creature on the face of the earth. Every physical idiosyncrasy was observed and faults were searched for which would usually end in a nick-name. The 'new' boy would, in his turn, become superior to all of those who would follow him, and he too would examine and search for faults; and in so doing, lose a little of his own inferiority to the stranger.

The 'baldy' itself made Thomas Kelly different from all the other boys and his eyes had surged with tears as he had 'run the gauntlet' of one hundred and fifty boys, his hair shaven to a prickly mass – exposing for all to see the two small smooth white bald patches at the back of his head.

Now, fourteen months later, as he crawled on all fours, following the scattered spots of wax, his resent-

11

ment and anguish was in no way diminished from that first time when Big Noddy had yelled – 'Right down on the floor, Patchy Heid!' and then had stood back smirking while the other inmates of the dormitory – well trained in how they should react when the 'donner' uttered anything faintly resembling a joke – rolled about, doubled in two and held their sides with laughter.

Even when his hair had grown dark and thick again, he remained 'Patchy' and had continued to suffer the humiliation of being the friendless recipient of numerous punchings, kickings and scurrilous remarks, in the infliction of which Saint Martin's had more than its share of experts.

The Chapel bell knolled a welcome relief to Patchy and he bundled the greasy dusters for washing before making his way to morning Mass.

With a religious intensity he hadn't experienced for years, Patchy Kelly beseeched God to help him and somehow end the unbearable degradation which had become his lot.

The dining room was large and appeared brighter than many of the other rooms in Saint Martin's. There was enough room to allow several small tables, each seating four boys, to be spaced comfortably throughout the hall. At one end, a two-tiered platform supported Gabriel's table and Gabriel himself, who now stood, arms folded, as the boys entered in double file and took up standing positions at their allotted places at the tables, where the porridge that the baker boys had served was already awaiting them.

No audible sign was necessary, a sharpening of Gabriel's expression being a command for silence. In a split second, it was obeyed and the mumbling and movements of a hundred and fifty adolescents ceased; three hundred eyes hit the floor, and a hundred and fifty voices chanted in unison:

> For the gifts we are about to receive
> May the Lord make us truly thankful   Amen.

The boys pulled out their stools and sat and chattered and grabbed at spoons and milk and napkins; there was a noise which had no crescendo.

But still Gabriel's eyes were watching – and being watched.

His presence dominated the room and even those boys seated at the furthermost corner of the hall with backs to him, knew instinctively when he issued a command, whether it was audible or unspoken.

The 'grubbers' were busy this morning. Gillespie anxiously awaiting an opportunity to be rid of his own porridge unobtrusively, felt his stomach somersault as he watched Dewar shovel the seventh plate of that slimy food into his large-sized mouth. How could he devour even one plate of the stuff? he wondered. The milk was sour and Gillespie, in common with ninety per cent of the lads, had grewed at the taste. Fortunately the 'grubbers' were in good form, and unwanted food could be slipped under the tables, to Dewar or Mallaney or Kerr who would refuse nothing and who vied with each other to see who could devour the most.

Dewar, a short podgy red-faced boy, was the present holder of the little contested title of 'School Grubber,' having earned his fame while at Auchterarder, where the boys spent three weeks of every year berry-picking. The food had been terrible, but, hard-working and hungry, the boys had managed to devour most of it until the day they had been served with a particularly disgusting broth. They all remembered how Grubber Dewar had poured the rotten tasting and even more disgustingly coloured soup down his gullet, loosening his belt as plate after plate was slipped beneath the tables to his corner. Dewar could refuse nothing and had consumed thirty-two plates, leaving his rivals far behind. Even on the morning of the 'moudie', Dewar hadn't let the boys down, and had indeed felt something of a hero, even though his heroic deeds were regarded with more than slight repulsion, by his benefactors. Gillespie continued pretending to eat, while watching for his turn to be rid of the porridge, and felt his stomach lurch again and the remaining colour drain from his face as he thought of the 'moudie.'

Six weeks before, a poor mouse had got itself drowned in the milk can and the dead animal had only been spotted as milk and mouse were poured into the tea boiler. It being impossible to retrieve it from the boiling tea, the mouse had been anatomically strewn throughout thirty-eight teapots. Even after being shown a severed tail, which had been rescued from one of the pots, Brother Gabriel, or Lucifer as he was known to the boys, had insisted that the tea be drunk. Few had managed to get the liquid past their lips, but Grubber Dewar had that morning added another notch to his belt of honour. Today, he was busy reinforcing his reputation with the sour milk porridge.

Gillespie, deep in thought, had failed to notice the approach of Lucifer, till he heard the voice at his elbow.

'You haven't eaten your porridge.'

'No Brother,' spluttered the boy.

'Why not?' roared the Prefect.

'The milk Brother, it's sour', whispered Gillespie, trembling in fear of the dreaded strap which he was sure would descend any minute.

'Bring it here,' ordered Gabriel as much to the boy's relief he moved away in the direction of the cupboard in the wall.

Gillespie immediately rose and followed and the other boys listened in amazement as Gabriel instructed him to leave the porridge on the shelf and return to his table, without so much as 'one of the belt'.

'What's Lucifer up to?' they speculated, though not for a minute did one of them think that the matter was finished or that Gabriel would forget.

They were still speculating when, with breakfast over, they were marched out of the dining hall to their respective jobs. And for some of them today's job would be picking tatties.

You don't spend fifty years on farms without developing your own meteorological office right there in your skull and Brian Flafferty's own little met. office told him that the remaining potatoes had to be lifted today. No doubt about it. That west wind whistling in his ears told him there was stormy weather ahead for the West of Scotland.

Cold and frosty it was with a thick white coat on the potato shaws. 'Right there,' his shrill Irish voice rang out, sending white clouds from his small, slightly twisted mouth. 'Give your dead carcasses a rattle and I

15

want every single spud lifted.'

The boys knew what was wanted and they rushed at the shaws tearing them with cold fingers from the soil. Thankful they were to see the last of the tatties.

'Get them Irish grapes lifted,' shouted Flafferty picking up a long twig and running ahead of the horse and harrow making mock swipes at the boys backsides. 'I'll soon get you warmed up.' His voice assaulted their ears.

Two boys there were to every six yards and the moment the horse passed their pitch they rushed in with their baskets plucking the potatoes with slightly more joy than they had plucked the frozen shaws. Up, down, back, forth, up, down . . . It was back-breaking toil for tourteen and fifteen year olds, untrained in the rigours of the farm.

'There's a moudie,' shouted McEwan, and four boys broke off to chase the mouse, whose entire world had just been torn asunder by the harrow. 'Never mind the bloody moudie,' roared Flafferty, taking three quick strokes at McEwan's buttocks the moment he reached the boy, 'And give yourselves a shake the rest of you. Get those backs bent or I'll bend them for you.'

Hard work it was out here in the fields, but hard work never killed anybody, and as for these boys . . . make men of them it would . . . all this fresh air and exercise of the muscles . . . liked his job in Saint Martin's did Flafferty . . . best job he had ever had and Flafferty had had a few in his day, working with pigs and cows and barley and pratties the length and breadth of Ireland and Scotland all his life . . . Finish his days in Saint Martin's, he would given a chance . . . Well it wasn't like other farming jobs . . . here you had all these sturdy young lads in your charge who could be put to

16

all the jobs you didn't fancy yourself and you were doing them good too . . . but these pratties would have to be in today . . .

'Scrape that soil clean,' he bawled, swishing his twig up and down the field, 'There's a tumshie for the best pair of you when we get this field cleared.' The boys gave themselves an additional shake at the thought of the turnip prize. But Patchy Kelly wasn't waiting to be awarded such a trophy; he was already in the next field where the large, juicy tumshies grew and had picked himself a beauty before Flafferty spotted him. 'Come here you thieving rascal,' he shouted, and Kelly, who had dropped the turnip, sheepishly approached the farmer. What excuse could he make? None . . . he would just have to take the punishment which Flafferty would undoubtedly administer . . . 'Bend over,' he heard the small Irishman shout, and was in the process of fearfully obeying when a mouse jumped from underneath a shaw twelve inches from his eyes. Patchy jumped, startled by the rodent and ran screaming to the derisive laughter of the other boys nearby, who nearly burst with fits of laughter at the sight of a big lad like Patchy screaming at a mouse. Flafferty made a rush at Kelly and bent him over. Patchy screamed again as the twig came three times into contact with the seat of his pants, and again the others laughed.

Now bend those backs and get those potatoes lifted,' roared Flafferty pushing Kelly towards his allotted pitch.

CHAPTER 2

From time to time the Marist Brothers would bid
farewell to the confines of Saint Martin's to enjoy a few
days of complete and utter silence during which they
communed only with God, praying and meditating over
the sins of mankind. It was during one of these Retreats
that Brother Gabriel had the idea of organizing a
One-Day-Retreat for the boys in the school.

The idea had delighted Brother Alphonsus highly and
subsequently brought from him a commendation to
Gabriel for his imagination and initiative. The other
Brothers had also been whole-heartedly in agreement
with the suggestion and the chosen date was now only a
few hours away.

The preparations necessary for such an event were
minimal – the main requirements were the participation
of the boys and a supply of suitable reading material
which would form the basis of their study and meditation on the great day. Weather permitting, the yard
had been chosen as a suitable venue.

Despite the simplicity of the programme and the
enormous amount of informal discussion which had
already taken place on the subject, Brother Alphonsus,
never one to leave anything to chance, had decided that
a meeting – which he would address – was essential in
order that final arrangements could be made for the
important event.

He spent a busy day preparing for the meeting. He
first drafted his speech, then he sent for the 'office boy'
whom he despatched post haste with letters to each of

the Brothers (excluding John) and also Father O'Rourke, requesting their presence in the staff room at seven o'clock in the evening. To Brother John had been allocated the duty of supervising the boys while the meeting was in progress.

Normally the staff room boasted a degree of comfort in the form of six large moquette-covered armchairs, where the Brothers could often be found relaxing, as the rigours of duty allowed. Tonight however, Brother Alphonsus, deciding that informality was not in keeping with the business in hand, had pushed the armchairs against the walls and erected a dark wooden table around which the five men now sat on hard upright chairs. At each place on the table, a large sheet of writing paper and a pencil had been set out.

Alphonsus himself graced the head of the table. To his right sat Father O'Rourke, and Alphonsus noted with pleasure that, although no doubt the Priest had indulged himself before arriving at the meeting, he was by no means inebriated. On the same side was Leon, looking very young and thin, but nonetheless keen and interested. Gabriel had taken his place to the left of Alphonsus and now sat upright and correct, showing on his handsome face, what Alphonsus considered to be the appropriate shade of solemnity. To Gabriel's left was Joseph, irritable and restless at what he thought was a waste of time – particularly as it should have been his night off.

'. . . . While all of them have been baptized into the Faith, the road to righteousness had for them had devious routes, each covered in the temptations of the devil.' Alphonsus, while making a valiant attempt to memorize his carefully written speech, found himself having to refer to his notes. 'Each of the boys in this

20

school has trodden the path of wickedness and each has finished his journey in a dead-end of damnation – an enticing lair of sin and evil which Satan had devised to trap the weak and straying. We, here,' continued Alphonsus dramatically, moving a hand towards those assembled, while now peering closely at his notes, 'under God's guidance, represent salvation to these sinners. In our hands we hold the key to the golden door, which, if we are successful, these boys may pass through and make their peace with the Lord in meekness and redemption. However difficult and ungratifying this task may be, we must continue – with the aid of God and by every means in our power – to turn these boys from their wicked ways and set them on the path of righteousness.'

Now that the bulk of the speech was over, Alphonsus thankfully abandoned his notes and continued in a more informal tone. 'Brother Gabriel, having the well-being of the boys in mind, has come to me with what I consider is an excellent suggestion. His idea, as you all know is that we have a One-Day-Retreat, not for the Brothers, but for those in our charge. I myself find this a most exciting prospect, and in my travels, both in this country and abroad, I have never at any time heard the idea mooted that a Retreat should be held for the boys. Excellent, excellent, Gabriel,' he said, now turning to the younger man and giving him a hearty slap on the shoulder, 'you must be commended for your foresight, excellent, excellent.'

Now to the arrangements. The Retreat will take place tomorrow, beginning immediately after breakfast. For the occasion we have purchased a hundred and fifty copies of *The Book of the Saints* and each boy will . . .'

While giving his blessing to the Retreat as being a purifying process for their charges, Brother John had not been looking forward to taking care of the one hundred and fifty boys of the 'Marty' while the meeting was in progress.

He had just spent a very happy day in Glasgow and had purchased for himself a new sports jacket and flannels and an overcoat. Unfortunately, lack of coupons hadn't allowed the addition of the pair of brown shoes which would have completed his outfit, but he had managed to get a beautiful leather hold-all. John had promised himself for years that one day he would treat himself to just such a case. Today he had achieved this ambition and he had been delighted. On returning to the school, he had been slightly nonplussed when he had discovered that a meeting was to take place, and the task of keeping an eye on the boys while the discussion was in progress had been allotted to him.

The setback, however, had only temporarily dampened his spirits and John's happy mood returned as he saw that the boys appeared to be quite settled in the main hall; some of them playing billiards under the impatient gaze of twice as many who queued for a turn, others enjoying a game of draughts or snakes and ladders, and the majority sitting quietly on the benches surrounding the hall engrossed in the mental consumption of an assortment of books, comics, magazines and other miscellaneous reading materials.

'. . . Ta ra ra ra true to thee till death.' John burst out aloud, unable to keep the music within himself. Encouraged by the Brother's outburst and prevailing good

22

humour, the popular hymn was picked up by Johnston Muir and Mason, who were seated nearby.

'Faith of our Fathers, Holy Faith, we will be buried in Dalbeth,' they warbled, at the same time emphasizing their devotion by stamping their feet, and banging the flats of their hands against the bench.

'Now boys, now boys, quiet — just a minute,' shouted John, taken aback at the unexpected turn of events and moving to and fro, waving his hands, as the song grew in momentum. My, he had been silly, he thought, constant vigilance and discipline were necessary with these boys. To him had been given the task of supervising, and if the situation got out of control, as could so easily happen in Saint Martin's it would appear as if he, John were incapable of handling the boys on his own. And what was worse, if the boys should sense any inadequacy whatsoever then the normal everyday control of them would become even more difficult. As the singing continued, the answer came to John. He would let them sing! Why not? He had organized concerts before, with smaller groups of course, and they had always been very successful, allowing the boys to exercise their exuberant spirits in the language of love and God, in song. Yes, this was certainly the answer. Without waiting for the noise to subside he caught hold of Carmichael, the store boy, and instructed him to bring a box from the store, strong enough to be stood on. John now moved amongst the boys until he spotted McAlian and taking the boy by the hand he walked with him to the front of the hall. The others sensing that something unusual was happening quietened long enough for John to inform them that they were going to have a concert and that McAlian would be the first to sing.

As Carmichael reappeared with the box, John stepped

23

on to it and instructed the now quiet boys to take seats on the benches around the hall. McAlian, a tall thin boy with an excellent singing voice of which he was justly proud needed no coaxing before mounting the box and, in a rich Glasgow soprano give his rendition of:

'At the cottage door one winter's morn as the snow lay on the ground,
Stood a youthful Irish soldier boy to the mountains he was bound,
His mother stood beside him saying you'll win my boy, have no fear,
And with loving arms around his waist, sure she tied his bandolier.'

As the boys happily joined in the second verse: 'Goodbye, God Bless you mother dear,' Brother John took the opportunity of making a quick sally to his own room where he collected his ukelele, returning in time to join in the applause as McAlain's song came to an end.

'Give us Cadogan – Cadogan for a song,' and as the chosen boy mounted the box which served as a platform, John stood beside him and accompanied Cadogan in his singing of:

'I was born in Boston City boys, a place you all know well,
Brought up by honest parents, the truth to you I'll tell,
Brought up by honest parents and reared most tenderly,
Till I became a Bouverie boy at the age of twenty-three.'

The boys, easily identifying themselves with the subject, softly echoed the singer's words and John, providing a background with his ukelele, found himself almost in tears at the pathos of the song:

'As I was standing at the gates, whom do you think I'd spy,
I spied my dear old father, a tear fell from his eye,
I spied my dear old mother, the tears came running down,
Saying John, my son, what have you done, you've been sent to Charlestown.'

Each thinking his own thoughts, it was a few seconds after the end of the song before the applause rang out. The concert was now in full swing and Rogan's version of 'The Big Mansion House called Barlinnie' was just the thing to provide amusement and change the mood of the audience. John was delighted, and even more so when Kelly, normally a quiet reticent boy, hestitatingly stood up. 'Yes, come on my boy, up you come,' he invited.

Patchy, considering that he had as good a voice as any and having at his disposal a vast repertoire of humorous songs, taught him by his father, decided that he would also sing a funny number. Climbing on the box, he began with the chorus:

'Noo, I didnae ken what tae dae,
Noo, I didnae ken what tae dae,
So I lifted my coat and walked awa',
I didnae ken whit tae dae.

One day as I sat on a dyke,
A wife she came by on a bike,

She fell in the mud, with a terrible thud,
Oh what a terrible sight.'

John himself, cheerfully tapping his foot and strumming his ukelele, joined in the chorus:

'Noo a didnae ken whit tae dae,
Noo a didnae ken whit tae dae . . .'

And again as Patchy took up the second verse, John merrily hummed behind the boy:

'Noo, I know a woman called Broon,
She took me into her room,
She took me on her knee and gave me some tea,
Mind you the gas was screwed doon,
Mind you the gas . . . was . . . screwed . . . doon . . .'

As the second verse was coming to an end, the accompaniment suddenly stopped two bars before the finish of the verse and Brother John grasped the astonished Patchy and dragged him from the platform. The final chorus of 'I didnae ken whit tae dae,' hopefully started by the audience petered out into complete silence which in turn gave way to giggling and laughing as the boys themselves caught the hidden meaning of the song of which poor Patchy still remained in ignorance and which John had only just realized. He was even more furious when he remembered how lustily he had participated in the first chorus.

John knew exactly what to do and Patchy's feet had scarcely touched the floor before he was directed to put out his hand, upon which he received two of the best.

Grasping the boy's sleeve, John made his way around

the hall until he spotted Clark, McLean and Reilly, three boys in his class that he had been specially tutoring to sing 'Like a Golden Dream' for the Christmas Concert. Directing the trio to the front of the hall, he hummed a note to give them their key and as the song got under way, he made his exit from the hall and along the corridor to the shower room, pulling Patchy with him. Thrusting the boy into a cubicle, he told him to have a shower while expressing regret that he was unable to wash out his tongue at the same time.

On his way back to the hall, John's ear caught the melody of the song now in progress. They must have finished 'Like a Golden Dream' very quickly he thought. What was that they were singing now? No! Yes, it was! A Protestant hymn!

The trio, whose repertoire wasn't confined to 'Like a Golden Dream' had scarcely waited till John was out of earshot before abandoning his chosen air. Young Reilly in the centre of the group had then announced;

'Brother John was been teaching us two songs for the Christmas Concert and we think you would prefer to hear the other one — now would everybody be quiet.'

After a few whispered giggling words amongst the three, Reilly again took up his stance on the box and the singers, hands crossed sedately in front of them, commenced to harmonize their party piece which Reilly had been diligently teaching them and which he himself had learned far from the walls of the Approved School — an unholy parody of 'The Church's One Foundation':

> 'The dogs they had a party, they came from near and far
> And some dogs came by aeroplane and some by motor car

27

They went into the lobby and signed the visitors
book,
And each one hung his arsehole, upon a separate
hook.

One dog was not invited and this aroused his ire,
He rushed into the meeting-place and loudly
shouted "fire."
The dogs were so excited they had no time to look,
And each one grabbed an arsehole, from off the
nearest hook.'

Every boy was now convulsed with laughter. Many
had heard the song before and some of them knew parts
of the verses. Some others had only taken in the one
offending word, but this combined with the present-
ation by the singers was sufficient and every boy in the
hall rolled about, helpless with laughter. John, reaching
the door was in time to hear the last verse:

'It is a sad, sad story, for it is very sore,
To wear another's arsehole, you've never worn
before,
And that is why when dogs meet, by land, or sea,
or foam,
Each sniffs the other's arsehole, in hopes it is it's
own.'

John too was almost in a state of collapse as the
words relayed themselves to his unbelieving ears. He
threw open the hall door and the belly-laugh was
immediately reduced to a few uncontrollable, hysterical
giggles.
   Stand up, stand up,' he spluttered promising to
himself that there would be no more concerts and that

at all costs, never again would the soprano voice of Kelly be heard within the precincts of the Marty.

He had always believed that 'evil begats evil,' and the night's events had certainly proved this to be correct.

'Come on, up ye get! Time for the 'can'. Come on, hurry up!' The 'Dandelion' dormitory was full tonight, thought Feeney, as he sauntered from bed to bed, shaking the sleeping boys by the shoulder, adding where he deemed it necessary, a quick sharp nudge or an additional shake or slap on the buttocks.

Bad boys these, he thought, all of them bad. Yet they lie there looking like innocent babes. 'Come on, up quick! Is your bed wet?' Feeney hoped he had again caught McRae, but no, McRae's bed was still dry. The first time he's had a dry bed in a week and the weather getting colder too. Funny!

As the boys tumbled and staggered out into the corridors towards the 'can' and queued at the four cubicles provided in the strongly disinfected and well-aired atmosphere, Feeney, not for the first time, wondered whether it would have made any difference to his young life if he had been given the same attention as these boys. Fifteen he had been before he stopped. Not that he would ever tell and nobody knew except that toffee-nosed sister of his; now married to a draughtsman and living in London.

His father, God rest his soul, had been a hard man. Brought him up the right way he had. Punishment! That was the only way to deal with the shameful thing. Every morning his father had come into his room before leaving for the pits. Feeney had most often been awake, lying in fear and trembling, awaiting the dreaded visit. His father would take one sure sniff and if in any doubt push his hand under the bedclothes; finding what he expected, he would pull the bedclothes from Feeney with one hand, while the other expertly loosened the thick miner's belt around his waist.

His father said the habit came from the Kerrigan side of the family, as none of his side had ever wet the bed. Feeney accepted that this was probably true. He couldn't picture a big, strong man like his father ever having wet the bed or anybody ever belting him the way he belted his son.

However, his mother had died before he was two and he had never been able to ask her. But his sister had never wet the bed; she must have taken after da, thought Feeney. She had certainly been his favourite anyway.

Pampered, he thought, as he watched the boys stumble back to bed. Bad boys too, all of them bad! Yet he had to get them up like this three times every night and get them to the 'can'. Pampered they were, pampered! A good dose of the belt wouldn't do them any harm. It had stopped him, hadn't it? All those lacings. Made a man of him, they had. It's what these simpering, shivering things needed – a good hiding.

They had been quick this time, he thought. Only ten past five and they were all back in bed. It's this cold weather does it. Stops them having a carry on; they only want back to bed.

But it would be no easy night. He still had Goodall to attend to. Another dirty bastard; but he could catch them. He knew the ones to look for . . . the regulars . . . but this Goodall, he'd never caught him before. But, by

30

God, he'd be on the lookout from now on.

It had been quite by accident, he had gone into the Dormitory Two . . . thought he had heard a noise, and probably wee Spence having a nightmare. Just as he was making his way up the dormitory, he had seen Goodall's blankets moving silently. As Feeney had pulled the covers off the bed, Goodall jumped up, looking as if he had been sleeping . . . they were all that fly . . . but Feeney knew what he had been doing. No use trying to pretend to him . . . he hadn't been night watchman in an Approved School for seventeen years for nothing.

Now he crept silently back toward Dormitory Two. At first glance he thought Goodall had gone but now as he looked closer, he saw that the boy was lying on top of the bed fast asleep. 'Get up you dirty scallop. Thought I told you to stand at your bed,' he screamed at the startled and frightened boy. Now all need for silence was gone and Feeney dragged Goodall to the door of the dormitory. 'Playing with yourself, were you? I'll show you where that gets you.'

Man and boy reached the dormitory door just as the small band of Brothers were making their morning journey to chapel.

Brother John, followed by the others, all passed unheeding, never for a moment raising their eyes as they apparently contemplated their feet and the cold stone on which they trod. Only the red head of Gabriel, who was Prefect in Charge, moved to acknowledge the existence of Feeney, and in his long white nightgown, the shamefaced Goodall.

'Playing with himself,' said Feeney. Brother Gabriel needed not one word more. Instinctively drawing the long leather Lochgelly strap from his sleeve he lifted Goodall's right hand and adminstered four of the finest.

Patchy Kelly lay in the corner bed of Dormitory Two listening and watching Lammy Goodall's predicament with intermingled fear and curiosity. Since the day he had entered Saint Martin's Patchy had lived in terror of Gabriel's leather belt, and it seemed to him as well as to others that he had tasted more of it than any other boy in the school. Scarcely a day had gone by without his being treated to the sharp sting of that dreaded leather across his hands or his buttocks. Now, his black head straining over the bedclothes, he watched Gabriel replace his strap, fold his hands, and walk off in the direction of the chapel, while Feeney, after instructing Lammy to remain in the corridor, headed in the direction of the night watchman's cubby hole and carefully closed the door behind him.

Patchy's feelings were indeed mixed. Being so often at the receiving end of Lucifer's wrath himself, he could sympathise with the other boy. At the same time he also experienced a certain glee that someone like Lammy could also find himself in the situation that had for so long now, seemed to be Patchy's natural born state.

He had long admired Lammy, both in the school and in the streets of Dalmarnock from which they both came, and where he was known as a real Gemmie. Big for his age and handsome, in a strong, hard fashion, he reminded Patchy of Errol Flynn, his favourite film star. Lammy always had plenty of clothes and cigarettes and gear like watches and lighters and money; all of which seemed to indicate to Patchy that the 'jobs' he did were paying off quite nicely. Yet he wasn't like the others who bragged stupidly about their activities. In addition, he was an uncommon success with the 'tarts' one or more of whom could always be seen hanging on to him. In fact Patchy could recall only one occasion when he

32

had seen Lammy without a bird and that was in the Brigton Billiard Hall where he was very much of a man's man; good at the cards and the snooker and the fighting, beating all others without any great effort. God, but Patchy admired him. And his admiration hadn't ceased when he had heard a month or so before he himself had been sent to the Marty, that Lammy had been shopped by Wee McCrindle and was in Saint Martin's.

But Patchy's admiration had never been rewarded and Lammy looked down on him as a 'cod' always at the lap up and showing off. 'Daft Patchy,' he called him.

But now, watching Lammy shuffling and rubbing one foot against the other in the cold corridor, he experienced for the first time in many months, a genuine feeling of pity for another, and saw an opportunity to curry favour with the best fighter in the place, the Donner of the school which was what Lammy had become on the day that Big Noddy had left.

Patchy rose and quietly crept to Lammy's locker, from which he brought forth the other boy's slippers. These in hand, he moved silently towards the dormitory door. Lammy, unaware of Patchy's presence till he felt something move behind him, turned startled.

'I thought you . . .' Patchy whispered.

'What do you want, ya Patchy heided bastard?'

Patchy smarted under the insult. 'A pity ye got caught wanking eh?' he spat out, throwing the slippers at Lammy's feet and making a quick dash towards the 'can'. But not before he had experienced the great delight of watching Lammy blush to the roots. By Christ, he thought, that's got him worried!

Lammy was worried. It was no more than a month since Big Carmichael and Malaney had been caught in a compromising position in the store. Brother Alphonsus had assembled the whole school in the main hall to deliver a lecture on the sins of impurity. No names had been mentioned, but none needed to be given when the boys were already writing slogans on the walls and passing bits of papers with verses on them from hand to hand, and when Big Casey Denver was rushing around the playground chanting:

'Grubber Malaney lay on the floor
Calling out for More! More! More!'

Lammy, as he now stood in the chilly corridor, all sleep gone from his mind, could still hear Brother Alfie's Irish voice ringing in his ears:
'I have been in many boarding schools, both in this country and in that great Continent of Australia, and never, never have I come upon such sinful deeds as those which have been perpetrated within these walls, by two boys who have dragged the good name of Saint Martin's in the mud . . ' Christ, Lammy thought, have I to go through that? But, maybe not. Maybe Lucifer and Feeney will forget it . . . maybe . . . but that Patchy heided bastard, he'll no forget . . . he'll blab it all over the school. Christ! He'll maybe even blab it all over Dalmarnock. He'll tell all the birds . . . Christ . . . I . . . I could go in there and batter his heid in, and make him forget it . . . but the Brother . . . Christ, it might stop me getting out for good in three months . . . I might get held up for a stupid bastard like that. Maybe I could lap him up? That's it, I'll lap him up.

Being dismissed, at least temporarily, from his punishment, by Feeney, Lammy entered the dormitory thirty minutes later to find Patchy in the act of taking the polisher and the bees wax tin from the cupboard.

'Fancy a shot of the polisher yerself, the day Patchy?' gruffed Lammy, scarcely able to look in the other boy's direction.

Noticing Patchy as he now stood, the handle of the polisher tightly grasped in both hands and the tin of wax under his 'oxter,' a group of boys gathered looking incredulously at the pair.

'Aye,' said Patchy, 'I'd thought I'd have a shot.'

A silence developed throughout the entire dormitory as the notion spread that here was Patchy challenging the donner of the school. It was queer altogether. Maybe Patchy was a dark horse who really could fight? Maybe he'd learned ju-jitzu or something. But, by God, he'd better be good – taking Lammy's polisher. They looked from Lammy to Patchy and back again in stunned reticence, waiting for Patchy to be felled and scudded the way others in the past had been almost slaughtered by Lammy.

It was a moment of crisis for Lammy, who, even after having decided the course of action to be followed was still torn between losing face with the 'home boys' and the thought that this silly idiot might go round Dalmarnock telling all the birds of the district about his shame. He spat on his hands and rubbed them together sending a shiver of excitement throughout the room, then grabbed a brush from Willie Creggan who was too terrified to utter a protest.

'I'll take this brush,' said Lammy roughly, astonishing the others and bringing a smile to Patchy's face. 'You have a go with the polisher, Tommy.'

35

Tommy! Tommy! Patchy restrained himself from crying out loud. Tommy . . . Tommy . . . that's what Lammy had said! Tommy! Tommy! Tommy! It rang through Patchy's head like a song – it was a song! It had a tune – it had a rhythm – it rang – it took sails and floated, took wings and flew – it took legs and danced all round his weary mind, lighting up the very darkest corners. He almost sang it aloud – Tommy . . . Tommy . . . Tommy! Tommy . . . Tommy, Tom!

It was by far the most beautiful word he had ever heard inside the school. With the staff it was 'Kelly' or 'you lad', or just a nod or a pointing of the finger. With the boys, it had been Patchy,' always 'Patchy,' as though they had been at his christening and heard the priest 'I now baptize this child Patchy' – as if he was supposed to like the name or as if they thought he was too stupid to know that they were referring to the two bald spots on his scalp.

But now all that was past – Tommy Kelly, who had ceased to exist in a Glasgow Remand Home, fourteen months before, had been reborn, and he was full of joy!

A proud and benevolent smile on his face, Patchy stuck out his chest and yelled to the others, 'Come on, hurry it up, we'd better get on with this or we'll never get done this morning.'

'Right Tommy,' came a chorus of voices; and it seemed to Patchy that some of his own joy had been imparted to them and never had the morning chores seemed such a happy event.

The brushers swept the dust methodically and a dozen of the lowly ones waited with floor cloths to fall upon their knees and rub in the wax which Patchy now skited in inch-and-half blobs, at one yard intervals, as though he had been doing it all his life. Patchy was enraptured; taller and more erect than he had ever been in his life. Now he almost danced along the dormitory floor with the bees wax. Then the polisher, the real hallmark of kingship, which he wielded to the rhythm of the song in his mind: Tommy ... Tommy ... Tommy! Tommy ... Tommy ... Tom! Never, he thought, had the floor been so bright or the workers so gay!

The challenge to Lammy's supremacy was an historical event and felt no less by Lammy himself. He was quieter than anyone had ever known him. He was humbled and worried, unsure of himself; and so preoccupied with his thoughts that he did not even hear the 'Hi Lammy,' that big Carmichael, the store boy gave him as he came into the dormitory with a fresh supply of bees wax.

Carmichael then spotting Patchy with the polisher, tossed the tin in his direction. 'Catch this, Patchy,' he shouted, feeling rather proud of his throw.

'Catch this PATCHY.' The words pierced Patchy's brain like an arrow. A flush of blinding rage filled his bloodstream almost to bursting point. He threw the polisher aside, caught the can of polish and returned the throw, aiming straight at Carmichael's head. 'My name's no' Patchy,' he screamed at the unfortunate Carmichael, who with a look of startled fear, managed to duck the polish tin which burst open as it thudded against the dormitory wall, sending its orange contents spattering in blobs and splashes over the fresh cream paintwork.

Goodnatured Carmichael stood aghast. Patchy had always been Patchy, what else was he supposed to call him? What the hell was it all about? As he turned to an enraged Patchy, he sensed that a different and more urgent problem now faced him, and he decided he

37

should 'flee the pitch,' disregarding the consequences of being dubbed a coward by these boys in whose minds brute force ruled supreme.

But he was too late and a wild and furious Patchy now fell upon him pummelling him with his hands, butting him with his forehead and groining him with rapid upward movements of his knees. 'Don't call me Patchy ... don't fuckin' well call me Patchy!' he repeated again and again as the bewildered, battered Carmichael resolved that never again would he do so and thirty other boys stood around making similar resolutions.

Lammy tried to pull Patchy off the wounded and bleeding Carmichael but found he was dealing with a boy with the strength of ten men, punching out all the frustration of fourteen months with the insulting nickname.

'Come on Tommy ... give over, he's had enough. You don't want to kill him,' urged Lammy, now really frightened and trying to grip Patchy's clothing in an attempt to pull him away from the battered Carmichael. 'Come on you'll get caught,' he said, gripping the tail of Patchy's cotton shirt which had now escaped from the top of his trousers. 'Come on, Fenney'll hear ye, he was outside a minute ago.' With this he gave an urgent pull at the shirt, which, coming away in his hand, sent Lammy staggering back against the dormitory wall.

When the story was later repeated, as freqeuntly it was, it was said that the thud of Lammy's body against the wall had knock down the crucifix, which now landed at Patchy's right hand. The truth of this is debatable, as the wall was of solid brick, but nevertheless the crucifix did indeed end its journey on the floor before being grasped tightly in Patchy's hand. Carmichael, seeing an opportunity of escape owing to the other boy's momentary distraction, managed to stagger to his feet and with every last vestige of strength stumbled his way along the corridor.

On nearing the door of the store, Carmichael drew the key from his pocket, turned it and when inside was about to relock the door, when Patchy pushed it hard from the outside.

Carmichael headed for the furthermost corner of the room, but not before Patchy had spotted him and hurled the wooden crucifix in his direction.

For the second time that morning. Carmichael's head had a lucky escape, and as he ducked, he had only time to notice that other figures had joined Patchy and Lammy at the open door, and that one of them had the bright red hair of Lucifer.

The Brother, coming up behind Patchy and Lammy, made a quick grab at the hair of the two boys and without waiting for an explanation, had started dragging them in the direction of the Prefect's Room, when from the corner of his eye, he spotted Carmichael at the back of the store.

'Get the other one Tom,' he shouted to Feeney, as he resumed his journey with the two captured boys.

The innocent Lammy was screaming in pain, but Patchy for his own strange reason was enduring the ordeal in utter silence, which did not go unwitnessed by the other boys in Dormitory Two, who now, as they saw the group approaching, flew back inside the dormitory, picking up dusters, polish, brushes and polisher, so that when Gabriel passed, he had a view of boys hard at work, like on any normal day.

Neither had Patchy's silence gone unnoticed by Gabriel, who, thinking that he must be losing his ability to inflict punishment, pulled harder at Patchy's locks, until with a final tug, he swung the two boys into the Prefect's Room, just as Carmichael, held in similar fashion by Feeney, also arrived.

After one look at Carmichael, Gabriel decided that whatever his part in the mêlée, he had been more than sufficiently punished, and with what was for Gabriel a gentle push, told him to report to the nurse and he would see him later.

'Trousers down and bend over that bed,' he roared, pulling the unfortunate Lammy by the collar and physically ensuring that his command was obeyed.

Lammy was almost crying before the first stroke of the belt descended on his buttocks. 'Christ what is going to happen to me next,' he wondered.

Lammy reckoned that he had always behaved himself with care and sense, if not always according to the rules, since entering Saint Martin's fifteen months previously. He excelled in sports and in work; there was nothing particularly bright about him, in any scholastic sense, but neither was he a dunce. Being 'donner' of the school since Big Noddy had got out for good, he had never experienced the host of petty abuses, which were the lot of the weaker boys during their incarceration. But now, within a few hours, his little eggshell was crumbling around him, exposing him to a world where he was a stranger and which he did not know or relish.

His sad thoughts were interrupted by half-a-dozen strokes of a strap, which the boys swore, and Lammy believed, Lucifer kept in vinegar for greater effect, and which now brought from his lungs, six screams, each of the first five as it died being reinforced by a further lash, driving fear and trembling into the huddled group of boys in Dormitory Two.

Pulling the unfortunate Lammy from the bed, Gabriel abruptly dismissed him and now turned his sharp, not unhandsome face, upon Patchy, who, for reasons best known to himself, sported a crazy grin and showed not the slightest sign of his usual fear.

Patchy had not been wrong in thinking that Lucifer had 'spite' against him. Scarcely a day had passed without Patchy being cuffed or strapped or made to stand in this corner or that for some misdemeanour or other. On one well-marked occasion, Lucifer had broken a school pointer over his back, and on every encounter, without exception, Patchy had been heard to scream. It was this screaming more than anything else that pained Brother Gabriel in his relations with Patchy, and in an effort to silence him, he would inflict more pain, only to be rewarded by more of the infuriating screams, and so on, creating a vicious circle, where Gabriel considered he had always come out the loser.

But today it was precisely that screaming he wanted the boys out there to hear, coming from Patchy's stupid grinning mouth.

Pushing him down upon the bed, he let go with the hardest stroke he could muster and waited, for the expected noise; but none came. Patchy, clenching his fists, his whole body tense, took the lash without any audible sign.

He too was aware that outside in the Dormitory, boys would be listening. Listening as he himself had done on so many occasions.

But his newly acquired pride kept the pain within him; it continued to serve him, and as each successive lash was answered with a victorious silence, his resolve grew, and he lost interest in counting the strokes; his whole body now concentrated on not crying out; and he

41

rejoiced in his silence, as this became easier and easier.

With each failure to induce a response, Gabriel became more and more infuriated, his strokes becoming wilder and wilder, until, blind with rage and anger, he drew the sharp leather across Patchy's limbs, immediately raising a bright ugly welt that stretched right across both legs, below the boy's knees.

A warning bell now rang in the normally methodical, if stoic brain of Gabriel. He had gone too far – what had possessed him?

Tired now and no longer able to cope, he briskly dismissed the aching but triumphant boy.

As the door closed behind Patchy, the precise and orderly Gabriel, Marist Brother and Prefect in Charge of Saint Martin's, threw himself across the bed, a tangle of infuriated and frustrated manhood.

Father O'Rourke was already past his best and far too fond of the altar wine long before being sent to Saint Martin's. Truth to tell, it was for this reason that he had been called upon to take charge of the souls of the delinquents assembled here by the joint efforts of the Glasgow Police, the Magistrates and the Catholic Education Authorities.

He was an incurable, though harmless alcoholic, safe from the public gaze within the walls of the approved school.

His offering of the Mass had never been speedy, but was now growing progressively slower, increasing the restlessness of his non-voluntary communicants, who by their very nature, were not the most fervent believers, having for the most part stolen their way into Brother Alphonsus's latest boarding school. As the Masses grew longer, so the twisting, turning and restlessness of the lads became more and more pronounced.

But not only were the boys impatient with this prolongation of the sacrament; the Brothers too were showing signs of nervousness and Brother Gabriel's enjoyment of the Mass was of necessity spoiled, for as prefect in charge of the lads outside school and working hours, constant vigilance was necessary, particularly when they were bored and nervy.

As Gabriel alternately kneeled, kissed his crucifix and responded to the Latin Chant as demanded, he reflected that seldom could be relax and wholeheartedly participate in the progress of the ceremony.

Today, the boys were particularly restive, and as Gabriel stood to repeat the Apostle's Creed he had a quick look around. Something wasn't quite right. As the congregation again took their seats, Gabriel quickly moved from his pew, genuflected at the end of it and made his way to the door of the Chapel.

From his vantage point, a quick count and an experienced eye told him that one boy was missing, and he hurried from the Chapel and made his way towards the dormitories.

His suspicions were quickly confirmed as beneath a bed in the furthermost corner of Dormitory Two, he sighted a small figure. A closer inspection showed him that it was Wee McRae, an occupant of the Wet Bed Dormitory, who now lay fast asleep, an open comic by his side.

Gabriel took great delight in aiming his leather strap at the boy's buttocks, bringing forth a startled scream, followed by: 'Sorry Brother, sorry.'

43

But Gabriel asked no explanations and proceeded to lash out with six of the best. It was while he was thus occupied that he noticed the orange bees wax splashes on the wall.

'Who did that?' he snapped.

McRae, who like every other boy in the school had heard of the 'big fight,' saw a means of escape from his predicament, but nevertheless cautious lest he be dubbed a 'shopper', was deliberately vague.

'Maybe it happened during the fight, Brother . . .'

'The fight?' Gabriel who had meanwhile been looking round the room was aware that something was amiss . . . 'And what happened during . . .' Suddenly he knew. The Crucifix! Yes that was it! The wooden Crucifix normally adorning the wall now spattered with wax was gone!

'The Crucifix, where's the Crucifix boy?' His whole attention again focused on the unfortunate McRae.

'I don't know Brother, honest Brother, it must have been the fight Brother.'

The fight, yes the fight thought Gabriel, remembering the scene at the store. Now everything was clear.

CHAPTER 3

Lammy's job as a bakery boy was not easy, but it was prestigious, and he was proud when on becoming an all day worker, he had gone straight into the bakehouse.

Kneading dough, pushing, pulling, filling and emptying trays before the hot ovens, and transporting by head the boards of bread and pies and sausage rolls and biscuits from bakery to kitchen and to dining room and ultimately to the tables, in addition to pouring the porridge and custard and soup, kept the boy busy, and there was little time for thought.

But it was a job to be proud of. If a baker took spite he could spit in a plate of custard, just for the hell of it; or he could prepare and serve a sausage roll with a piece of wood in it, in place of sausage meat.

If you were 'in' with a cobbler boy, he could arrange for you to get a slightly better pair of boots and a tailor could fix you up with a less patchy and ancient jersey or socks, for your 'all weekwear', which could boost your morale, and make you feel less miserable than a lad, who say landed with a jersey, the original wool of which had been entirely replaced by darns of shaded, or even different coloured, wool or worst of all, with only half sleeves.

But a bakery boy! Well, he could affect your stomach, and if he took spite, could all but poison you.

So, contemplating the power which still remained to him, Lammy had, while pouring the porridge, felt a slight restoration of his pride, and was regaining some of his self-respect as he distributed the loaves to the one-hundred and fifty boys assembled in the hall. But moving hither and thither between the tables, he became aware that Gabriel's eyes had settled permanently upon him. For the first time, he felt the disadvantage of being a baker boy. Not for a minute could he escape the full force of those eyes. When eventually, the loaves distributed, he was returning to the kitchen, empty breadboard in hand, he scarcely needed the crooked finger of Gabriel to indicate that his presence was required at the top table. All hope and fight now gone, the dejected Lammy obeyed with a meekness about which he would never boast to his grandchildren, should he live long enough to have them.

Gabriel slowly and deliberately rose from his seat, raised his arm and wordlessly pointed a finger at the now expectant Carmichael and Patchy, who like soldiers on a parade ground, instantly obeyed the command. Gabriel patiently awaited their arrival at the foot of the platform and then beckoned all three up the one step which placed them on level with him in front of his table.

Savouring the silence, the Prefect allowed them the few moments necessary to sight and recognize the wooden crucifix which had once adorned the wall of Dormitory Two; and now lay stark and affective on top of a white sheet of blotting paper. No attempt had been made to fit the parts together, the white paper accentuating the gap which had appeared between the upright and the crosspiece.

'Collect your porridge and bring it over here,' invited Gabriel, for once in a soft, but recognizably menacing voice, indicating one of the two empty tables at the foot of the platform. As the boys returned in record quick time, porridge plates in hand, he beamed in their direction. 'Eat up now boys,' he said in a tone which might, to a stranger, have been reminiscent of a kindly mother chiding her erring offspring.

An expectant hush had fallen over the dining hall and it was something of an anti-climax, as Gabriel, apparently no longer interested in the three choking boys, turned his attention to the solitary figure of Gillespie standing to the left of the dais. Obeying instructions, the nervous boy had been standing there alone from the moment breakfast assembly had begun.

Recalling events of the previous morning, the boys had again speculated what Gillespie's fate might be. Hard luck, poor Gillespie getting caught like that just as Grubber Dewar was ready to take the porridge from him. But even the other grubbers had been hard pushed the previous morning, as very few of the boys, even those who didn't have Gillespie's delicate stomach, had managed to push down the lumpy porridge with the sour milk. 'Bet he gets six of the belt.' 'Taken to the Guv.' 'Maybe they'll make him scrub the yard,' ventured a new boy with a sense of humour, who on entering the school a few weeks before, had been subjected to the normal teasing: 'Go to the store and collect a tin of tartan paint and a glass hammer,' and had been told that his first duty would be to scrub the yard.

'Don't be daft. No. I'll bet he loses his privileges. Gabriel hates it when anybody doesn't finish the grub.'

'Sure, if he takes him to the Guv, that's what'll happen – "all privileges must cease" ' – mimicked

Thomson, putting his hands behind his back and dropping his head in a fair imitation of Brother Alphonsus.

'But why did he make him put the porridge in the cupboard,' questioned McInnes, more astute than the others.

Gabriel himself had been brought up to 'clear his plate,' his great grandfather having lived through a famine; that his grandfather, father, and eventually Gabriel himself had never been allowed to forget. To Gabriel the wastage of food by sinful souls like these boys, who after all were here for punishment, was as bad as the crimes most of them had committed to get here in the first place.

Gillespie, and all witnessing, had to be taught a lesson. 'Bring out the plate of porridge,' the Prefect said, indicating the cupboard at the side of the hall, where he had the day before instructed Gillespie to leave the uneaten meal.

The boy hurried to obey, completely at a loss as to the reason. In the past twenty-four hours, he had wondered many times what his punishment might be, with always at the back of his mind the nagging thought that the porridge was still in the cupboard in the wall.

Attention was now focused on Gabriel as Gillespie returned to stand before him plate in hand.

In the voice which he reserved for command, the refusal of which, the boys were sure, would bring about instant death, Gabriel dramatically produced a spoon from behind his back, held it out to the trembling Gillespie and roared, 'Eat up that porridge!'

Three hundred eyes, including Gabriel's were fixed on the boy as he attempted to eat his porridge of the previous day. With each spoonful of the terrible concoction, he grewed even more than the previous morning but he was under Gabriel's instructions and there was no question of disobedience. In a valiant attempt to comply, he pretended to himself that it was in fact Sunday, that he was home, that in his right hand he held a spoon and in his left a plate of custard and apples; that this was just a bad dream which would pass away in seconds. As he pushed down spoonful after spoonful of the totally cold porridge with the milk even more sour and discoloured than it had been the previous day, his normally ruddy face grew gradually whiter and whiter, as the eyes of one hundred and fifty boys were upon him.

Gabriel, seated on his dais, cut off the tops of his two boiled eggs more nonchalantly than most people in Britain would have done in those war-years when eggs were strictly and severely rationed. Certainly the boys before him, who had seen only two eggs apiece in the past twelve months, would have tackled them with relish. The head cook considered that the number of eggs produced by the combined efforts of a hundred and sixty ration books and the school hens was inadequate for even distribution and, practically on the day that war was declared, had decided in her wisdom that it was more sensible that the Brothers and the Staff should have a couple a day and that the lads should have maybe one at Easter or thereabouts than that she should attempt the futile task of equal distribution on a daily, weekly or even monthly basis.

Gabriel's eyes, taking in the whole scene, were savouring with pleasure the consternation on the faces of the three boys seated at the front table. Let them wait, he thought gleefully, given them time to turn it

49

over and over again in their minds, and contemplate
the punishment ahead of them.

Carmichael, his left eye blackened and bruised, was
absorbed in a general aura of unhappiness with the
events of the past two hours, and too listless to think
of Lucifer's intention. Lammy was troubled in case his
run of bad luck would extend to a longer stay in Saint
Martin's, but Patchy, even with his buttocks, thighs
and calves burning and swollen from his severe tan-
ning, still managed to wear a strange look of content-
ment which troubled Gabriel as he slowly wiped his
strong jutting chin with his chequered napkin,
munched his toast and sipped his black coffee.

It was Patchy of whom he was thinking when he
noticed that Gillespie had done with his porridge, and
beckoned the latter to him with curled finger.

'You enjoyed that, didn't you?' he clipped, and the
ashen-faced Gillespie, nodded, struggling for words.

'Ye ... ye ... yes ... Brother,' he said.

Gabriel surveyed the room with a sly, triumphant
look, and was about to dismiss the boy when Gillespie
involuntarily started forward and released a quarter
gallon of vomit, over the remains of the eggs, the
crucifix and blotter and down the right side of Gabriel
to end its journey, a white-yellow, undigested mass in
the lap of his black Marist habit.

After a moment's awed silence, there was a great
burst of laughter from every boy in the hall intermingled with a roar from Gabriel. As he jumped from
his platform and onto the main floor of the hall, the
laughter which had now reached dimensions of
hysteria, just as suddenly ceased and all was still.
Gabriel's furious and tormented eyes saw only one
face, that of Patchy, seated with the other two boys

at the front table. Gabriel lunged towards the boy and had already delivered three strokes when he heard from the other end of the hall, loud, defiant and clear, the one word 'Spite.' Forgetting Patchy, he turned his immediate attention in the direction of the caller, and as he rushed towards the other end of the room, his leather swinging from his soiled hand, the chant was taken up, slowly and deliberately at the right of the hall – 'Spite . . . spite . . . spite.' Then to the left, 'Spite . . . spite,' the one word, beginning softly, and as Gabriel thrashed about the room, increasing in slow, intense, determination, and echoed by every boy in Saint Martin's, 'Spite . . . spite . . . spite . . .'

Brother John bounced his way through Brother Joseph's classroom towards his own, where on a normal weekday, he would be teaching the top class. His small, round, red figure normally had an aura of jollity and during spasmodic spurts of energy he could be heard singing to himself 'There's a beautiful lady called Eileen O'Grady . . .' his favourite solo. This morning however, his genial nature, which had been sorely tried by the events of the previous evening, was having difficultly in asserting itself.

Carrying the half of an apple which he had taken from the kitchen, he was headed for the feeding of his budgie.

'Beetjie, beetjie, beetjie,' he cheeped, rising on the tips of his toes to press the apple between the wires of the cage, which hopefully, he kept high out of the way of his pupils, who were not above having a bite at the daily apple. It was because of this that he had developed the habit of bringing the fruit early of a morning when the boys were at breakfast, to ensure that the budgie had at least a few stabs at the succulent meal.

The budgie was tweet-tweeting back with obvious relish and gratitude when John's eyes noted that his corner blackboard had been interfered with. Someone had dusted away 'Like a Golden Dream'.

'Like a Golden Dream', he had been teaching every day of his eleven years in Saint Martin's, and one of his greatest joys was in watching the twenty-odd young toughs who constituted his class following his pointer, as he strutted up and down before them leading them in:

> 'Like a golden dream, in my heart ever shining,
> Lives the vision fair of happy dreams, I knew in days gone by . . .
> Can my dreaming be in vain, will my love ne'er come again,
> Ah, come shall we waste the golden hours of youth far apart . . .'

John, while he would never condemn the use of the strap or even underestimate its value as a disciplinary weapon, and indeed could wield his useful length of leather with as much expertise as the rest of the Brothers, felt that in order to divert at least some of these untamed young criminals from tripping the well-walked path from Saint Martin's to Borstal to Barlinnie and Peterhead; they should have a goal at which to aim.

Many years ago he had decided that 'Like a Golden

Dream' was the necessary instrument to soothe the savage breasts of those wayward adolescents, while at the same time illuminating the beauty and joy of life. To this end he had diligently and patiently taught the song to every person who had passed through his class, and, as in the case of Clark, Reilly and McLean, he had taken groups of boys he considered promising and had spent much of his free time giving them special tuition. 'Have I been wasting my time?' he thought, recalling the events of the previous evening, 'After all I've done for those boys, to be rewarded like that.'

On his first day at St. Martin's, back in the hungry thirties, Brother John had on this very blackboard, painstakingly and lovingly, with thick white crayon, inscribed for all to see, the chorus and two verses of 'Like a Golden Dream'. On reflection John doubted if a single word remained in its original state. It had so often been vandalized that he doubted if any part of the previous writing had existed for more than three months.

Most often it was just a word or two which was obliterated, to be replaced by one or two choice words from the culprit concerned. Sometimes a whole line would be erased and replaced, but today, it was the complete song that had been effaced, which suggested that the culprit had been interrupted at his work, and had no doubt intended to chalk the words of some disreputable song or chorus of which these boys appeared to know hundreds.

That was it! It was Kelly. Obviously he was the type of boy who would finish up selling dirty post-cards, thought John. Kelly, he had already decided, had been responsible for the fiasco of the previous evening. Kelly it had been who had channelled the proceedings in the direction of filth and pornography. Brother John had been pondering the wisdom of reporting the happenings to Brother Alphonsus and had almost decided against this, believing that he himself should be able to handle the situation. But this new effontry! Maybe he would be wise to have a word with the Governor. No, he would challenge Kelly. He would ask him if this indeed was his revenge, and he would be able to tell at once from his face whether he was innocent, or had indeed vandalized the blackboard.

No matter how it turned out, there would be little use in making the boy rewrite the song on the board. His writing, even with pen on paper was almost illegible, and 'Like a Golden Dream', had to be plain and clear and easy for all his pupils to read and to sing and to carry with them for the rest of their days. He would have to rewrite it himself, and to this end, he climbed laboriously onto a chair.

Scarcely had his chalk begun to grace the blackboard when the outburst of laughter from the dining hall assaulted his ears.

Something's wrong, thought Brother John. Brother Gabriel wouldn't have them laughing like that. Wish he would! He had often chided Gabriel for not taking things a little easier. 'Come on up with me and see the Celtic,' he had again and again encouraged the younger man on a Saturday afternoon. But no. Gabriel had declined. He pushed himself too hard, thought John. He was a good, dedicated man, but you could be too dedicated, and a man had to relax in some way or other.

The noise continued, and John carefully replaced his chalk and thoughtfully made his way to the dining hall. Here the noise clarified itself, and he could make out the slow monotonous chant of 'Spite . . . spite.'

Gabriel was standing at the bottom of the dais, facing the boys and making no attempt to use the leather which was hanging from his limp arms. He stood stock-still, his face deadly pale and completely bewildered. As John approached he noticed the stains stretching the length of Gabriel's black gown. Sensing immediately that something was very far wrong and that Gabriel was incapable of dealing with the situation, John spoke quietly to the younger man.

'You'd better get yourself cleaned up, Gabriel, and I'll take over in here,' he said gently, pointing to the now silent boys.

'Thank you John,' said Gabriel, who turned and quietly left the room.

Brother John now focused his attention on the three boys at the front table. Bouncing up to Lammy, he challenged him first –

'Why are you here?' he snapped in his Yorkshire accent.

'I don't know, Brother,' replied Lammy.

'And you?' John now turned his attention to Patchy, who likewise shook his head, as did Carmichael.

'Hold out your hands,' Brother Gabriel didn't have you sitting here for nothing.' Lifting his leather strap he administered two strokes each to the trio, who were beginning to feel as though there wasn't a square inch of protective skin on their entire bodies.

Noting the sickly appearance of Gillespie, who again stood at the side of the platform, John decided that this boy appeared to be more sinned against than sinning and with a nod of his head indicated that he should take the fourth seat at the front table.

Before finally dismissing the assembled boys, Brother John motioned them to be upstanding as he led them in the 'Grace After Meals'.

'We give thee thanks, Almighty God, for all Thy benefits, who livest and reignest, world without end. Amen.'

Spite on Kelly? The accusation was utterly unfounded and unthinkable, Gabriel told himself, as he discarded his soiled and tainted clothing and filled the bath with the cold water of winter.

Didn't he know only too well that spite and revenge were sinful things and far removed from his mind and his very soul? Hadn't he seen Kelly laughing louder than any of the others? And wasn't this the reason he had strapped him? Spite, he thought, there wasn't an ounce of spite in his bones. Kelly had done wrong and Kelly had to be punished.

Scrubbing and soaping and rinsing himself again and again, he prayed to God to lead him in all his dealings with these unfortunates.

It had only been because of the sour-milk porridgy vomits on his habit that there had been a momentary lapse of his authority, he thought; and as he soaped and scrubbed in the ice cold bath – which to Gabriel was as great a cleanser of the spirit as of the body – his confidence soon returned and he knew that he could restore his hold over the boys of Saint Martin's. He asked God to guide him in his attempts to find and punish the sinner who had desecrated the crucifix, and as he donned his fresh habit, he felt himself once more clean and pure.

'Brother Gabriel, Brother Gabriel, a moment please,' called Father O'Rourke as he sighted Gabriel leaving the bathroom. 'Were you not feeling well this morning Brother?' enquired the little Priest in his rich Kerry brogue as he followed Brother Gabriel into his room.

'I never felt better in my life, Father,' said Gabriel cautiously, wondering if the Priest could possibly have spoken to Brother John about the events of the morning. 'Why do you ask?'

'Well, when I saw you rise and leave the chapel, during the Mass, I was wondering if perhaps...'

'No,' Gabriel looked down into the priest's chubby face. 'I noticed that there was a boy missing and went to investigate.'

'Oh, so that's what it was; and did you find him?'

'Yes,' replied Gabriel, 'in one of the dormitories.'

'Dodging Mass?' said the priest, unsurprised.

'I'm afraid so,' said Gabriel, hinting, 'some of them do get restless, Father.'

'I'm sure they do,' said the priest, too long in the horns not to ignore the inference, 'and sure, I remember as a boy doing the same thing myself, I'm ashamed to say.'

'Surely not Father?' queried Gabriel.

'Yes, I'm afraid so, and more's the shame on me,' shaking his head with more than a trace of amusement, 'but there's something else, I've been meaning to ask yourself, Brother Gabriel,' proceeded the little Priest cautiously, 'I notice, and very pleased I am to see it, that you take Holy Communion every morning...'

'Yes, Father,' interrupted Gabriel, now fully in

command of himself, 'I never miss the Sacrament.'

'Yes, yes, Brother Gabriel and grand that is to be sure, but the funny thing is that I don't seem able to recall the last time you were at Confession,' said the puzzled priest.

'Yes, Father, that is correct, and there is a very simply explanation,' said Gabriel, 'I never commit any sins, Father.'

'You never commit any sins!'

Gabriel chose to ignore the look of astonishment which crossed the Priest's face.

'No, Father, I don't.' Gabriel was now his old confident self. 'At one time, I went to confession regularly and always began by saying, "Forgive me Father for I have sinned," but time and again when I examined my conscience, I would discover that I hadn't committed any sins . . .'

'You hadn't committed any sins!'

'No, none at all, Father, the only sin I was committing was telling the lie in the Confessional, saying that I had sinned.'

'Now now, Brother Gabriel, "the just man shall fall seven times a day," and you're telling me that you never commit any sins at all? You know, even to think sinful or impure thoughts is every bit as bad as the actual commission of a sinful deed . . .'

'Yes, Father, I am fully aware of that fact, but I take the greatest care to lead an utterly blameless life,' said Gabriel, turning and pulling out his handkerchief in a polite attempt to bring the conversation to a close.

'Well, well,' said Father O'Rourke, his sense of humour now asserting itself, 'and not another day must I be wasting before writing to the Holy Father in

Rome and preparing him in advance for your canon-isation. But in the meantime, I must be about my duties, so I'll bid you farewell.' With this he turned and left the now somewhat perplexed Gabriel to his thoughts.

As the door closed behind the Priest, Gabriel won-dered what the duties could possibly be to which the priest referred.

Gabriel's own ambition, as yet unrealized, was to be an ordained Priest, and here, he thought was Father O'Rourke, who having achieved this great ambition seemed to be putting it to such little use, fumbling his way through the Mass every morning and with such a terrible effort that the Brothers constantly feared a recurrence of the awful occasion when during Benedic-tion he had stumbled and fallen on the altar steps, much to the amusement of the boys.

Gabriel had no wish to be unkind to Father O'Rourke, but in common with the other Brothers and boys of the school, he had concluded that the weakness which had caused this collapse had been due to plain old-fashioned drunkenness, and more than likely, the duties to which he now referred were connected with the bottle.

Sure, what other duties, did Father O'Rourke have? he thought; a Benediction every other month, Confes-sions on Friday afternoons; and even at them he had been known to fall asleep while listening to the stories of the boys.

Gabriel, whose duty it was to sit in the Chapel and watch the boys as they made the way to and from the Confessional, well remembered the occasion only three Fridays before, when his attention was drawn by the more than usual restlessness of the boys to a realization that it had been a considerable time since the last sinner had deserted the end of the pew for the confines of the Confessional. He decided to investigate, only to discover that McCarthy had finished his confession in the first few minutes, and had spent the remainder of the time waiting for Father O'Rourke to awaken from his drunken sleep to prescribe penance.

This was no way to fulfil duties, reflected Gabriel, and now here was Father O'Rourke today, with all his imputations of impurity. Most of these Priests seemed to be obsessed with the problems of impurity thought Gabriel, no doubt having come about by listening to all the stories of infidelity and perversion while in the Confessional.

Just as a Doctor deals only with sick people, so of course a Priest is dealing only with sinners, with their tales of infidelity and adultery. And as a Doctor seldom had contact with healthy people, so a Priest will only infrequently meet hale and holy people like himself. Will-power, that was the thing, together with an ability to distinguish between good and evil and thanks be to God, he Gabriel was endowed with a goodly proportion of both!

The Devil reared his ugly head in many guises. Only recently thought Gabriel, if I had been a lesser man . . . that little laundry maid, Agnes. A bad young woman . . . all bursting at the seams, with huge breasts for such a small body . . . probably pregnant already . . . pushing herself against him . . . teasing, laughing at him . . . Cheap! But she had failed, and she was gone now and a good thing too . . . no place here for a girl like that.

And Sister Tierney, she was not so young, and not so obvious, but there was something about that woman. Gabriel recalled that on every occasion he had found it necessary to visit her room, he had come away embarrassed and shy. Like a little naughty boy. She was quite sure of herself and went about her duties apparently unperturbed at the thought of being surrounded by so many males. Yes, there was something about her indeed. She seemed somehow smug, thought Gabriel, as if she had discovered something about you which you didn't quite know yourself.

CHAPTER 4

Patchy unscrewed the tiny wall mirror and stood unblushingly manipulating it behind him with his left hand, trying to catch a glimpse of the back of his head in the big hall mirror, while wth his right he caressingly stroked the comb again and again through his thick dark locks.

He smiled conceitedly as he noted that the two offending bald patches were almost completely covered by his thick mop. Christ, he thought, with his newly acquired confidence, why did I worry about two wee things like that?

Often during the past months he had come to imagine that those patches were six inches in diameter. Now they were nothing.

'No bad, no bad,' he said aloud, angling the back mirror from left to right and totally unmindful of the other boys milling around waiting their turn. Some feigning disgust, moved off to crowd about other mirrors at the end of the hall, but none dared to hurry Patchy or disturb his self-admiration.

'Gees, they're some marks on your legs, Tommy,' was the only type of comment with which he now had to contend and while he dismissed them with a nonchalant shrug, they were like sweet music to his ears. He felt, and he had become, something of a hero.

Even Sister Tierney had seemed sympathetic towards his bruises, which she had spotted as he had been kneeling scrubbing his allotted portion of the stone corridor outside the Sick Bay. Her remark,

'Come and see me at four o'clock Tommy and I'll put something on those legs of yours,' had caused much amusement amongst his scrubbing companions and had given rise to more than one suggestive remark, all of which served as a stimulant to Patchy's newly found ego and though he himself never doubted that her interest was purely medical, this did not stop him joining in the general merriment.

'Hey Tommy,' shouted Lannigan, interrupting his thoughts and his admiration of the back of his skull, 'can I get that mirror after you?'

'Just hold yer weesht,' said Patchy, turning a wicked, forbidding look at the offender.

'O.K. Tommy, I'll use this one over here,' and Lannigan moved off to fight his way to the front of the group at the nearest mirror.

Changed days, was it thought Patchy, since he had first stood before this very mirror on his second day in Saint Martin's with his baldy haircut. But now fourteen months later, Patchy was far from feeling humiliated. He had publicly challenged Lammy, the present donner and he had beaten up a lad two inches taller than himself; he had also taken a hiding from Lucifer without flinching, bearing on his legs the signs of honour in the form of two vicious welts. And he was now known as Tommy. Yes! Patchy had gone for ever!

Even Carmichael's urgent shout of 'Quick, Lucifer wants us in the shop right away!' did not effect Patchy's new found self-assurance.

'What the fuckin' hell, does he want?' he spat out, as he swaggered along the corridor to the Prefect's room where Lammy was already standing to attention before Brother Gabriel.

'Right, stand up straight.' commanded the Prefect and Patchy and Carmichael quickly obeyed.

'Which of you broke the crucifix?'

Christ! The Crucifix, thought Patchy, suddenly recalling his sacriligious deed.

All three boys were silent.

Gabriel had a fair idea that Kelly was the culprit, but he wanted an admission and had decided that if he got one, he would minimise the punishment to a few strokes. But if no confession was forthcoming, then . . . .

Again he looked from one to the other.

'Was it you?' to Lammy.

'No Brother,' said the boy uneasily thinking that it was up to Patchy to confess and at the same time convinced that he would.

'Carmichael – you?'

'No Brother.' whimpered the lad, still physically suffering from his recent beating.

Brother Gabriel now turned his sternest gaze upon his chief suspect to find a defiant Kelly gazing sternly back at him.

'One of you three broke the crucifix,' he said 'and I would far rather have the admission from that boy's own lips than have to seek out the guilty party on a second-hand basis. Kelly?'

'No Brother.' said Patchy, not unaware of a slight shuffling of feet from the other two.

Fearful lest Lucifer's strong right hand was about to bring down the leather band of justice upon their ears, the three boys twitched and shuffled about, until, surprised they were led outside by Brother Gabriel.

'Stand there,' he commanded, indicating a position in the corridor, 'and don't move.' and with this he turned in the direction of Brother Alphonsus' office.

65

'Sacrilege!' howled Brother Alphonsus, his normally gentle nature giving way to anger as the tale unfolded. 'Sacrilege, Sacrilege.'

'I believe that Kelly is responsible,' said Gabriel.

'And I too am of that opinion.' As he spoke Alphonsus gazed back and forth at his own crucifix set in the wall in front of his desk.

'All three must be punished until the culprit confesses,' said Alphonsus now reaching a decision, 'and the whole school must be taught that this will not be tolerated. These three must be separated from the others and all privileges in the school must be suspended until one of them confesses.'

This was exactly what Brother Gabriel had expected from the Governor and yet he flinched slightly. It was easy for Brother Alphonsus to sit there and take such a decision, but it was he, Gabriel who would have the responsibility of seeing that the sanctions were imposed, and the memory of the last two boys who had been ostracized was still fresh in his mind.

Geaton and Brown had absconded and almost broken the record for 'jollers' from Saint Martin's. Worse still, the story had reached the National newspapers and as a consequence, the usual belting, baldy haircut and loss of privileges, were considered by all the Brothers to be insufficient and it was decided that the boys should be ostracized by the entire school. This had had a cowing effect in both cases, as Geaton, by nature a quiet boy, had become a complete introvert, and Brown, a bright outgoing lad, had physically wilted before the eyes of the school.

In itself it had been a necessary punishment Gabriel thought but Brother Joseph's subsequent action could have resulted in very serious consequences.

66

Gabriel recalled that it had been, and still was, a habit of Joseph's to choose, not enemies but close friends as partners in his boxing tournaments, which in the first few moments usually led to the boxers sparring gently with each other. But a few taps on the ears and a tugging of hair by Joseph usually put an end to such play acting.

Gabriel remembered how the whole school had gasped when Joseph had chosen the ostracized Geaton and Brown for one of his bouts.

The boys had patted and feinted at one another, scarcely even pretending to punch, when Joseph had swooped wildly upon them administering smacks and cuffs and pushing them apart, before calling them to battle again. But their cuffs merely grew gentler and gentler, and again Joseph slapped and pushed them apart, then insisted that they fight, to no avail until the two boys eventually didn't even raise their hands, but just stood and looked at each other. Joseph in frustrated despair had finally demanded that the boys remove their gloves, and to murmurings of 'That's a liberty' had administered six strokes of his belt to each, before ordering them to bed.

As Gabriel now listened to Brother Alphonsus elaborating on the punishment for Patchy, Lammy and Carmichael, he determined that nothing like that would ever happen again and would indeed have questioned Alphonsus' ruling if he had an alternative to offer.

But he had exhausted his armoury on the recalcitrant Kelly, at least for the morning, and besides Brother Gabriel believed in bending in obedience to his superiors in the same way that he expected the boys to bend in obedience to him. So he accepted the decision, if reluctantly.

Gabriel rang the school bell with additional vigour which to the boys was the first indication that something special was in the offing. They made their way to the Main Hall and lined up in their four Houses in double quick time, with only Tonto making any chit-chat.

Tonto was ignored by Brother Gabriel, who, knowing that any command would have been disregarded, at the same time felt sorry for the little boy who imagined he was the Lone Ranger, and for whom he himself, in a moment of great compassion, had carved out a wooden gun with which the boy could run around the play-ground firing at imaginary enemies. But even Tonto soon quietened in the ominous atmosphere.

Gabriel, having established complete silence, was standing facing the boys, with eyes that saw every movement of the lip, while commanding unease in every heart. The Governor entered, ushering before him three boys.

Indicating that Patchy, Lammy and Carmichael should stand at the front of the congregation, the Governor now took Gabriel's place in the centre of the hall.

'I have been in many boarding schools,' he began and even Gabriel had difficulty in suppressing a smile as Alphonsus continued with his oft' repeated speech, 'both in this country and in the great continent of Australia, and never have I come upon such evil, sinful deeds as those which have been perpetrated within the walls of this school ... by the deliberate and wilful destruction of a crucifix. From this moment until the culprit owns up and confesses, by his own tongue, all privileges are cancelled.'

The last two words were lost in a sea of shuffling

68

feet and murmuring lips... 'The bastard... we'll be kept in on Sunday... no more pictures on Saturday ... they'll stop the night biscuit... Christ, they might even keep us in at Christmas... the bastard.'

Gabriel's eyes now joined those of the Gov's in restoring a deathly hush.

'As to these three boys, one of whom has dragged the good name of this school in the mud, they will eat and sleep, wash and work apart from the others until the culprit has come to me and confessed. Until that happens, not one of you will speak to any of them, unless you have been specifically instructed to do so, by either myself or one of my staff.

'This morning and for the rest of the day, we will be having our "retreat" as planned, during which time there will be no talk outside the Dining Room. While meditating and praying to God, I would ask you to offer special prayers for this school and to beseech our Lord to forgive this terrible blight upon its name.'

With one last long, stern look at the three principals, Brother Alphonsus left the hall. The closing of the door behind him signalled a gale-force wind of expletives which made the three boys tremble visibly and which Gabriel allowed for a brief moment, wishing he could have allowed it to continue. But the retreat was his very own idea and it had to come into operation, even if it did momentarily relieve the three boys from the wrath of one hundred and forty-seven who had lost their hard-won privileges.

With a sharp command, which the boys claimed sounded like a News-vendor's 'Final', silence again returned to the Hall and he despatched six boys to fetch one hundred and fifty books on the lives of the Saints.

Now that the great moment had arrived, Gabriel was delighted.

The weather had been his biggest problem, and he had dreaded the thought that had it been raining, it would have been necessary to crowd one hundred and fifty urchins from the Gallowgate, Govan, The Gorbals, Tradeston, Bridgeton and Springburn into the confined space of the Main Hall with instructions to keep absolutely silent, reading the life of the Saints. But God had provided a dry, if somewhat cold and dull day, and so the boys had been ushered into the playground for their hours of prayer and meditation.

Gabriel stood on the steps of the main entry and proudly surveyed the spectacle of the boys settling down on the steps and benches, or walking slowly around the yard, each on his own, reading the sweet little books of the Angels and contemplating perhaps the miracle of Saint Denis of France who, moved by the spirit of God to defy his tormentors and prove his goodness, had walked around bearing in his blessed hands, his head, which had been severed from his body.

The scene was marred only by little Tonto, who had great difficulty in concentrating on a book, not one word of which he could read, and who, much to the amusement of the others, had an occasional rush around the yard shouting 'Tonto.' Gabriel after several such distractions, instructed McLusky to bring the boy to him and when two or three attempts to subdue his troubled spirits had proved unsuccessful, managed to

70

get Tonto a book with pictures.

The Prefect had solved the problem of 'Cartwheel' Cairney, the piggery boy by allocating him some gardening chores during the Retreat, as otherwise his cartwheeling would have upset the quiet and peace which was the basic prerequisite of the whole business. Cairney was an incorrigible who could suffer no more than fifteen minutes of silence without doing half a dozen or more cartwheels. Reading and writing were foreign to the boy, who had been sent to the Marty as being beyond parental control. On his first day in the school, Brother Gabriel had begun to understand why the boy had been so designated. The class of boys he was teaching at the time had settled down quietly to adding up a string of sums when suddenly the new boy had stood up at his desk, walked to the front of the class and performed three cartwheels to the right, and then three to the left; after which he had sat down to a great outburst of cheering and applause from his new classmates.

As it had been a unique and completely baffling experience, Gabriel had let the matter go until ten or fifteen minutes later when Cairney again stood up, came to the front and performed a further three cartwheels, the proficiency of which Gabriel could not fault, but in response to which he could see no alternative but to grab the boy by the hair and drag him screaming to the classroom door, which he dutifully did, returning to silence the giggles of the other boys with a single glare.

A few moments later Gabriel had to rush into the corridor because of the noise without, only to find that the cause of the laughter and applause he had heard, was the new boy's cartwheels, which were now

71

taking him down the corridor and into the yard to the great satisfaction of a group of 'baker boys', who could do nothing but admire Cairney's acrobatics.

After a few inconsequential beatings, Gabriel concluded that the reason that Cairney did cartwheels was that he could do nothing else and had recommended that he be put in charge of the piggery.

As the morning wore on, Gabriel caught sight of Sandshoe McLaren, whose powers of concentration were notably limited, drawing the attention of any who glanced in his direction to his paper-eating and nose-picking tricks, apparently not at all interested in the higher things of life.

And he watched with satisfaction the slow progress of Kelly, Carmichael and Goodall as armed with scrubbing brushes and buckets of soapy water, they continued their allotted task of scrubbing the huge playground.

It was sad, reflected Gabriel that they had chosen such a morning for their sins; such a day for their sacrilege! But they represented no more than a small blight in seven years of plenty, a tiny cloud in a clear blue heavenly sky and Gabriel shrugged aside his displeasure as his own blue eyes surveyed the scene of blissful quietude.

Fortunately the boiler room was out of his sight and pleasantly it was out of mind, or the spectacle of McKinnon the boiler boy roasting mice might well have upset his peace of mind.

Gabriel had a love of animals of every species and

the idea of anyone roasting rodents would have horrified him beyond description. But for McKinnon, it was one of the few real joys in life; between shovelling coal nuts into the glowing door of the furnace, adjusting gauges, having a quick drag of a fag and of course catching the animals, he roasted mice, toasting the screaming little creatures to death, tying their tails with wire and hanging them over a tin he had fixed up over the furnace door especially for the purpose.

Occasionally a couple of boys would break off from their meditative perambulation, sidestep into the boiler room and join McKinnon in his pleasures, some even being given a shot at holding the wire while McKinnon searched his pockets for fags or dog-ends.

An enterprising lad was McKinnon, an entrepeneur of the first great flood. He always kept a goodly supply of cigarette ends which he could barter for 'night's biscuits' of which people owed him thousands.

This biscuit was the last communal pleasure of an evening in the Marty, and also the great medium of exchange, even sausage rolls and pies were measured in so many units of the biscuit. It was sweet and wholesome and melted in the mouth.

Bela Lagosi, the white-haired Baker Man was proud of those biscuits and rightly so, and had he been as enterprising as McKinnon, he would have left Saint Martin's, set up shop outside and made himself a million, tickling Britain's palate with Lagosi's Night Biscuits. But his best customer would surely have been McKinnon, who loved them only second to roasting mice, and for this reason he was called the 'Biscuit Boy'.

Within minutes of the Retreat beginning, McKinnon had seen the opportunity of earning some more biscuits. So, setting up his own private library, he started distributing dog-eared Dixon Hawke detective novels. These were pocket sized and fitted easily inside the *Book of the Saints*, which each boy had been given and could thereby remain invisible to Gabriel as they were carried around the yard read by avid eyes; for each book McKinnon had the promise of a biscuit.

When he had run out of his own supply of Dixon Hawkes, he bought more for half a biscuit a time from others who had come prepared with their own literature. So renting and exchanging McKinnon was having a field day.

But McKinnon had a further interest that day, one which also coincided with that of Brother Gabriel and this was the squeezing of a confession from whichever of the three had 'desecrated the image of the Crucifix.'

'A'm no losing my privileges for any bastard,' the biscuit boy could be heard exclaiming again and again, while roasting his mice, puffing his fags and distributing his books. 'We should go right over there and kick their heids in, the bastards . . . You're gonnae lose your Sunday oot and your pictures for they bastards.'

There were none to argue with him, everyone who came near the boiler room was in agreement. But all of them knew that Lammy could fight, and Patchy . . . well that was some tanking he gave Carmichael; and these facts caused considerable hesitation.

The biscuit boy guessed that Gabriel wouldn't object too strongly if a few bloody noses were distributed to the culprits and that he might turn a blind eye to such persuasive endeavours. Often in the past 'jollers' had been punished by lads whose privileges were threatened. The biscuit boy well remembered

74

many occasions when he and a handful of others had smashed up the jollers, though usually they were new lads and smaller.

This time it was slightly more difficult: for one thing Lammy was the ex-donner and for another Daft Patchy was claiming the crown. 'But still, no bastard's gonnae stop my privileges,' the biscuit boy said again and again, until he had a dozen boys waiting for Gabriel to turn away.

They waited and they watched!

To have been aware of such happenings would certainly have been unpleasant, but there was nothing to mar Gabriel's delight as he cheerfully greeted Brother John who appeared to relieve him temporarily in his invigilation.

'Well, well, things are looking most delightful,' said John as he bounced towards the younger man. 'Marvellous, marvellous,' he enthused, as his eyes circled the yard. 'I'll relieve you now Gabriel. Matter of fact, just spoke to Sister Tierney and she mentioned that she wanted to have a word with you. Mind you I don't think it was urgent. 'My, my, this certainly was a marvellous idea,' and Brother John gave Gabriel a friendly pat on the back to express his delight. 'Off you go now, boy, and have a cup of tea to yourself and I'll look after things here . . . no hurry now . . . no hurry.'

John, immediately entering into the spirit of the project, slowly wandered round the vast playground, first reading a part from his sacred book and then raising his head to heaven and closing his eyes, better to meditate on that which he had just absorbed. He was completely unaware of the increased restlessness which had been heralded by the 'changing of the guard'.

75

Lammy moved closer to Patchy with his bucket and scrubber.

'You'd better tell them it was you.'

'Aw shut your fuckin' mooth,' snarled Patchy, in no mood for surrender.

'You'll get us all kept in, and it was you that did it.'

'Maybe you'll shop me eh?'

'I never shopped anybody in my life,' said Lammy wishing to himself that he could plant his bucket right over Patchy's head.

'Do it now, and I'll shop you to the whole school and all over Bridgeton,' said Patchy, pleased, as he saw the guilty blush spread over Lammy's face.

Both were unaware of the approach of McKinnon, together with another dozen boys that he had successfully whipped into a frenzy.

'Look out,' shouted Carmichael, bringing Patchy and Lammy to their feet with scrubbing brushes in hand. Patchy immediately ran for the crowd of boys, swinging his scrubber without aim, but catching three of the vanguard and frightening most of those around him. But it was Lammy who really put the tremble on the lips of the would-be attackers.

He had been expecting just such an event and had correctly guessed where its source would lie. Ignoring the rest of the boys he went straight for McKinnon and gave him a quick doubler on the stomach and a powerful jab on the eye which sent the leader of the onslaught scampering back, in the general direction of his scattering troops, and further retreating to his boiler house.

The three were suddenly close together and alone.

'We sorted they Bum Boys,' cackled Patchy.

'Aye, but they'll be back,' said Lammy. 'Just you wait till tomorrow when they don't get to the pictures, or Sunday when they don't get out for the day.'

With these words, the three boys fell into a deep troubled silence and while they continued with their scrubbing, cast anxious glances over their shoulders at the others who had returned to their Retreat.

Brother John, blissfully unaware of any disturbance, continued his walk round the yard, and between reading and meditating, thanked the Good God for the success of this Blessed Day.

Gabriel's high spirits continued as he made his way through the school towards the kitchen. All the frustration of the early morning now gone, he was elated at the success of his venture.

Who knows, he thought, it could possibly be taken up in schools all over the country and perhaps might someday be known as Gabriel's Retreat.' Even Brother Alphonsus, who had taught in many countries . . . had never heard of a Retreat for the pupils. And what a success it was.

Gabriel had decided that he wouldn't see Sister Tierney this morning. He would leave it until later. The woman irritated him . . . probably it was about Kelly's legs . . . why should he have to explain to her . . . and in any case he didn't want Sister Tierney or anybody else spoiling this day for him.

On entering the kitchen he found to his dismay that Sister Tierney was already there on the same errand as himself, and as he went forward, she turned towards him, startled.

'Well, good morning, Brother Gabriel.'

'I was just looking for a cup of tea,' said Gabriel casually, at the same time moving off in the direction of the cook.

'Why, I've got a pot here, all ready, I'll get you a cup . . .'

'Oh, right then, thank you very much,' Gabriel could see no way out of the situation.

'Perhaps you wouldn't mind having it next door with me and we could have a little chat. As a matter of fact, I'd been looking for you today to have a word with you.' Sister Tierney now placed the extra cup and saucer on her own tray and prepared to walk off with it.

'All right, yes, that would be nice,' muttered the thoroughly reluctant Gabriel. 'Here, let me take the tray.'

During the two years that Sister Tierney had been at Saint Martin's, Gabriel had on several occasions been in the nurse's room; sometimes he was called upon to describe the earlier symptoms of a sick patient or was escorting one or other of the boys for treatment. He had never failed to feel ill at ease, but never more so than this morning as he followed Frances Tierney through the front room with its desk, cupboard, instruments and medicines to the little room beyond, which was her sitting room.

The only time he had ever seen this room before was through the open door of the outer room, and as he now entered he thought how different it was from anything he had ever known before.

His own home in Ireland had been a dark, austere

farmhouse, the atmosphere similar to that of Saint Martin's, and his present sleeping quarters were not at all unlike his bedroom at home.

But Sister Tierney's room seemed to be full of light. The walls had been brightly painted and there was a rose patterned carpet covering the greater part of the floor with a small green rug in front of the fire, which she now prodded into light and warmth.

'Here, put it down here,' she said indicating the tray, at the same time pushing forward a small coffee table to sit in front of the large settee. As Gabriel bent to lower the tray, his elbow brushed along the side of her body and as he raised his head, he was painfully aware of his scarlet face and tingling nerves.

'God blast the woman,' he thought.

Sister Tierney, apparently quite unconcerned, sat down on the couch, lifted the teapot and proceeded to pour the hot tea into the two cups. 'Milk and sugar?'

'No,' he replied, unable to force himself to add 'thank you.'

Gabriel, still standing was at a loss. Where could he sit? Unless he went back into the other room and brought out a hard wooden chair, he had no alternative but to join Sister Tierney on the sofa. Not that it wasn't big enough for two, or indeed three or four, but such close proximity to the woman terrified him. However, he must look foolish standing like this. And feigning a casualness which he certainly did not feel, he lowered himself into the couch.

'Biscuit?' Gabriel shook his head and noticed that this was the second time she had addressed him and failed to add 'Brother Gabriel,' which further embarrassed and annoyed him.

Was this woman out to compromise him? he wondered, but she looked so cool and unconcerned, maybe he was judging her harshly, but of course she was a nurse, she was accustomed to men, she would be aloof in their presence, she had nothing to learn, there was nothing she didn't know about men. Gabriel felt himself blush again. Dear God. He wished that the ground would open up and swallow him. All his earlier joy now gone, he sat, thoroughly miserable, and felt like a puppet being dangled at the end of a string by this woman, who seemed to be able to look casually into his eyes and bare his soul.

Gabriel focused his attention on the tea in his hand.

'It was about Kelly . . . those marks on his legs . . .' Reluctantly he dragged his eyes from the brown liquid in his hand to look at Sister Tierney, but on the journey upwards as his eyes came into line with her breast, he once more felt the tell-tale colour rising to his face.

Sister Tierney moved further back into the depths of the couch and once more checked that the skirt of her nurses uniform was a decent length below her knees. She really had made a mistake, she thought. Why on earth had she ever invited Gabriel to her room. She had wanted to speak to him about Kelly's legs, and when she had seen him in the kitchen had thought that this would be the perfect opportunity and that the difficult subject would be easier broached in the friendly atmosphere of her own room rather than in the dining hall with the kitchen staff moving back and forth. Now she realized just how wrong she had been.

Before coming to Saint Martin's, she had given much serious thought to the unique problems of working and living in such an establishment and decided that a professional aloofness, coupled with good common sense and respectable well-fitting clothes and uniform would enable her to fulfil her duties as befitted a decent Catholic nurse without stifling the humane feelings which were common to her profession.

The boys, she had thought, would be her biggest problem, but as she had learned to ignore the whispered sniggering comments of her young patients, and had adopted a friendly motherly attitude towards them, she had experienced no trouble whatsoever.

The Brothers, she had realized would be something different. Accustomed as she was to the often deliberate crudities of thirty men in a hospital ward, the only knowledge she had of the purposely celibate male was old Father Connor, her Parish Priest, who, while he had been a great comfort to her, after her husband was killed, and had visited her alone in her home every other day until she came to Saint Martin's, could probably not even remember what a sexual urge was; she was therefore totally devoid of any knowledge of the sexually potent, but deliberately celibate young male, such as Gabriel.

Frances Tierney was now beginning to realize the enormity of her action in inviting Gabriel to her room. Being honest with herself, she would admit that on first meeting him, she had immediately been attracted to this handsome, redhaired sturdy young man. But, being aware that not for him were the delicious, titillating joys of even an abortive flirtation, she had quickly dismissed this from her mind and eventually came to see him, as perhaps he was, a man amongst children and a child amongst men.

Now, however as they sat at either end of the large sofa, she in her white starched uniform providing a sharp contrast to Gabriel in his long black robes, she was worried. Perhaps on looking back she might be amused, but now her sole determination was to get this interview over quickly, and nip in the bud this awkward relationship which she herself had created.

'Kelly's legs, they look quite bad, Brother . . . I was worried . . . if an inspector had come . . .?'

'No need to worry on that score Sister Tierney,' said Gabriel brusquely, 'The inspectors are fully aware of the difficult job we have . . . and in any case it's only eighteen months since they've been and we do get a few days notice of their arrival.'

'And is that the only consideration, Brother Gabriel?'

'No, indeed not!' Gabriel now replaced his cup and saucer and stood to go, 'You haven't been here long, Sister Tierney, but as you are no doubt already aware, the duties of the staff in this school are of an unusual and extremely difficult nature, and we must all pull together. You will find, that, as each of us have come to realize, criticizing our fellow members of the staff in no way eases our task, but, on the contrary . . .'

'Yes, Brother, I understand. In any case they should be alright in a couple of days. He's a big strong boy . . . I'll put some cream on them . . .'

CHAPTER 5

Endowed with a great love of youth, Mr Kavanagh, who worked on the building sites by day, devoted his spare evenings, which were usually seven a week, to touring the Approved Schools in the West of Scotland giving lessons in Irish dancing to those there assembled. Tonight was one of the two-a-week which he spent in Saint Martin's.

A man of enormous stature, the three fingers missing from his left hand did nothing to detract from his bulk. The disabled hand still resembled a good sized shovel with which he continued to knock out a fair old tune on the 'Squeeze-box'. This he began to do immediately on entering the main hall where he was confronted by the hundred and four boys, which by his own special request was four more than his normal quota.

Hearing of the crucifix being maliciously broken and of the three suspects, he had made straight for the dining room at tea time to talk to Brother Gabriel. A table had been set aside under Gabriel's pedestal and it was not difficult for Kavanagh to recognize the culprits.

'These are the three I've been hearing about, Brother Gabriel?' Gabriel nodded, wiping his lips with his napkin. 'If you wouldn't mind, Brother, I'd like to have them in my dancing class tonight – though I'd need another one to make up a set.'

'Take your pick,' said Gabriel as the musician's eyes travelled the room.

Kavanagh, a firm believer that punishment had a law of its own which declared that it was never without just cause, and that even then, was usually underdone, decided, on noting the bruised face of the 'biscuit boy', that this was the lad to complete his foursome.

'I'll take McKinnon,' he roared.

So it had been settled, and so it was that these four were to be found in the hall as he entered it.

Without uttering one word, he struck up a nameless Irish tune, which always in his mind brought forth memories of happy wakes and weddings and multifarious parties in the hills of Donegal where he had learned most of his music. But the same tune had different associations in the minds of his 'dancers' who recognized it as the signal for 'on the hands down,' which meant doing press-ups on the floor.

As the music began, one hundred and four boys fell to the linoleum and began the painful process of pushing themselves up and down to the rythmn of Kavanagh's favourite tune.

'Tum, tum ... tum ... tum ... tum ...' The giant hummed to himself as he squeezed and twiddled joyfully.

It never took many minutes before some boy weakened and fell to the floor and on this occasion the first to flop was McLusky.

Without missing a single beat of his music, Kavanagh hummed and danced his way lightfootedly towards the miscreant, stood astride the haunches of the slightly-built lad, and while his left hand continued to vamp the tune, his right administered what he called 'the McGinty', which consisted of a punch on the kidneys from his fearful knuckles.

The effect of McLusky's collapse was that of a 'cough in a crowded Chapel,' and as Docherty and then Robertson and then Mains collapsed, Kavanagh danced and hummed his way towards them and each in turn received the McGinty. As the boys continued to fall, the music continued to play, and each as he fell received his McGinty; and as more and more fell, the music became wilder and wilder, and Kavanagh's dancing got faster and faster, but yet, not a beat did he miss, and not one of those deserving it, failed to received the McGinty, and so it continued, until Kavanagh, in his wisdom, decided that he had tamed at least some of the wilder spirits.

The 'Siege of Ennis' was a formation dance, one of Kavanagh's favourites, and usually the highlight on School sports day, when the display was one of the most spectacular events.

Sports Day was held in June and was always a happy day. There were apple tarts and goodies galore. The visitors were treated to races and pipes and drums and colourful marches, and of course, Kavanagh's dancers.

The only cloud on this happy day, covered the thirty-odd boys, who were Kavanagh's 'ladies', who much to their humiliation were forced to dress as Irish Colleens, with short green silk skirts and blouses, purple sashes across their shoulders, white stockings and black pomps, and the whole ensemble crowned with an emerald bonnet, complete with hanging ribbons of green, white and orange. But 'ladies' were necessary, as was the 'Siege of Ennis' and Kavanagh certainly enjoyed himself.

Now as Kavanagh struck up the first few bars of 'the Siege', the boys in the hall ran to take up their

85

allotted positions, and while continuing his melody, the big man lowered the tone to enable Patchy, Lammy, Carmichael and McKinnon to hear the instructions: 'You four make a set here,' as he indicated with his head, a position directly before him.

The 'Siege' now commenced in earnest as the sets of non-voluntary participants, danced and jigged and bumped and tripped; and the 'ladies' who made up half the company, passed crude remarks, and received cruder ones, and gesticulated and pointed their toes and swung their hips and all endeavoured to cover their embarrassment.

The terrified McKinnon now found himself a vulnerable fourth to three on whom he had led his abortive attack.

'I'm sorry about what happened the day, Lammy,' he whispered as the two boys faced each other in a 'Paddy Bar'.

'Right – all stop,' roared Kavanagh, the whispered conversation being exactly what he had been expecting. 'You four on the "hands down." The rest of you, back!' As one hundred boys gratefully sank down on the benches around the hall, Kavanagh placed the four principals around him and struck up with the nameless but not unfamiliar tune. 'Tum... tum... tum... tum... tum...'

Up down, up down, up down, went the four, and Patchy was the first to receive the 'McGinty', followed by a sand-shoed toe, prised into his stomach, forcing him up to start again. 'Up down, up down, down, McGinty – up again – down again – McGinty again – up – down – McGinty – up!' So it continued for fully five minutes, until the four lay flat, and the hundred on the benches, all whispered conversation forgotten, sat silently with heads bowed.

Despite his exhaustion, McKinnon did not sleep as readily as usual that night. He had sworn revenge on Patchy — convinced that the other boy would never admit his guilt and so all would be deprived of their Saturday pictures and Sunday out, and maybe even the Sunday morning sausage-roll breakfast. McKinnon schemed and planned until every sound had ceased, save his own breathing. Then rising from his bed, he made his way to the Dandelion Dormitory to which Carmichael, Lammy and Patchy had been moved for the period of their stay in Coventry.

Now standing over Patchy's bed, he brought down upon the sleeping boy's nose, a tightly clenched fist. With delight he watched the bright red blood spurt from the other boy's nostrils before tip-toeing back to his own well-laundered sheets.

So it was a bruised and battered and forlorn Patchy who pulled the blanket all the way over his head that night, to weep and pray and wonder.

CHAPTER 6

The graffiti reflected the poetic genius, recorded the comings and goings and bore witness to the sexual fantasies of years of Marty boys. A more recent scratching gave the news: 'Malaney is a Bum Boy.' But it was of no particular consequence to Patchy when 'Cairney' came into the Home, (when 'Lynn' was due out for good) or who was the 'easiest bit of stuff in the Calton'. His interest in the 'can' door lay only in the momentary protection it provided from the hostile world in which he found himself.

The fact that a certain amount of silence had been imposed on the entire school the previous day had prevented the three boys feeling the full impact of the ostracism. But today was Saturday, when the school would normally be taken to town for an outing to the pictures and Patchy's isolation was complete.

Rubbing the bees wax into the stained wooden floor, washing up, sitting through Mass and then breakfast ·and all the time looking around, hoping for a smile or a nod or a wink of sympathy, he had only found eyes turning away from him.

He was no longer the hero of the previous morning, nor even the 'Daft Patchy' of the past. He was the nothing of his first days in Saint Martin's, and even lower, because then there had at least been some element of recognition. Now, he felt of another species, a lowly crawling creature burrowing holes beneath the ground, and the bleak, pine-smelling 'can' to which he had retreated provided cold comfort.

He remembered how, rather than be 'out on a limb', he had joined the other lads in Dalmarnock as they roamed the blacked-out streets breaking into shops. And now his activities had led him to precisely that 'out on a limb' position which he had tried to avoid. Even Lammy and Carmichael had now lined up against him.

The 'can' door burst open and the tall, threatening figure of Lucifer interrupted his thoughts.

'Right outside – quick,' he snapped and Patchy realized that he had overstayed his allotted time.

There was still no friendly face to greet him in the playground where the boys were assembled; and the faces grew decidedly more and more unfriendly as the day wore on towards picture time when the threat of 'no privileges' would become a reality.

Walking alone round and round the yard, trying unsuccessfully to believe that he was in some faraway happy land, he noticed McKinnon at the head of a group of boys gathered outside the boiler room. As he continued again and again round the yard, he saw the crowd grow bigger and bigger and ever more menacing. He pretended not to see, fixing his eyes on the concrete below him, until McKinnon broke off from the crowd to stop him in his tracks.

'Kelly, do you no think it's time ye gave yerself up?'

McKinnon's tone of friendly earnest pleading by no means fooled him. And looking from McKinnon to his forbidding 'army' he knew that he would be torn apart like a chicken if he did not respond.

Without replying, he turned and walked directly over to Lucifer who was standing on the steps towering over all he surveyed and no doubt waiting for just such a move.

90

'I broke the crucifix Brother,' he said, looking at the ground and bracing himself for whatever punishment lay ahead.

Gabriel stepped forward and with a triumphant look around the yard, pulled a whistle from his pocket and blew two shrill blasts which brought forth in a great scurry, the army of boys that had, with the exception of Sandshoe and Tonto, been watching the death march of Patchy.

Seconds later, they were standing still in their four double rows before the Brother whose blue eyes scanned the face of each and every one.

'Wash-room and good suits,' he snapped and a great howl of delight arose. 'And no talking.' Curling a finger at the front rank, he turned and pointed to the building.

As each boy passed Patchy, they patted him on the shoulder. 'Good old Tommy' or 'Good on you,' they said, and not one of them called him Patchy.

Whatever punishment Lucifer might inflict, Patchy was ready to accept, even if it meant he himself being kept in on Sundays and holidays or having his flesh bruised again by Lucifer's leather.

He stood where he was, waiting and alone, but not so alone as he had been three minutes before.

It was fully twenty minutes before Gabriel returned to curl his finger towards Patchy who obediently followed the big man along the corridor towards the Prefect's room – till he noticed the bright reflection of the object clutched firmly in Gabriel's right fist – a pair of barber's clippers!

Seconds later he was across the yard, down the path, over the wrought iron gate, through the fields, over the next gate and down the main road. Running;

running, running as no athlete had ever run — unless driven by a similar terror or a powerful drug — passing a man in plus-fours, who had scarcely time to consider why he was there or where he had come from, before he was past him, running on and on and on.

CHAPTER 7

The tram had gone six stops before the conductress approached for his fare.

Patchy pretended to go through his pockets and then looked up with pleading eyes, to notice that the woman was sceptically regarding his ragged jersey.

'Could you take my name and address?' he pleaded.

She eyed him suspiciously. A newcomer to the route she did not know of the Approved School two miles away, but one look at the ragged jersey had convinced her that there must be some sort of institution nearby and that this coatless, swarthy, brown-eyed boy was undoubtedly from it. But she liked his eyes.

'Where are you going, son?' she asked in a warm, sympathetic Glasgow voice.

'Into the town.'

'Here. Take that ticket in case the inspector comes on and whatever you do, get rid of that jersey.'

'Thanks a lot missus. I'm . . .'

'I don't want to know where you're from, son.'

'Just remember and change that jersey quick.'

The distance between stops seemed to lengthen. As more and more people boarded the tram, Patchy tried with greater and greater effort to appear inconspicuous. Looking out of the window and holding tight to his Godsend of a ticket, he was delighted that he had been able to induce such a favourable response from the conductress.

In the centre of a queue waiting to board the tram

in Rutherglen Road, Patchy spotted a policeman, who, on climbing the stairs, seated himself in front of the boy.

Patchy quickly sidled from the seat and off the tram as it was drawing to a halt at the next stop. He walked briskly through the nearest tenement close, and on exiting at the back of the building, smiled with relief as he saw that it gave way to half-a-dozen back courts, each one sporting several washing lines which were gaily covered with a miscellaneous assortment of towels, bed linen and wearing apparel.

Patchy noticed with joy that the lavatory at the back of the close was open and quickly made use of this. Being careful to keep himself hidden, he scanned the washings, and finally caught sight of a likely replacement for his own wear — a light blue jersey and a nearby yellow shirt.

A stout woman wauchled out from the next close and made her way towards the open stone midden where a black cat nosed inside a sardine tin only to discard it six feet from the pile of refuse from where it had come. A newspaper covered the shallow pan of ashes which she bore in front of her. Patchy watched as she picked her way between the dirty puddles, carefully manipulating her pan to ensure that it didn't touch her neighbours' clothes lines, while the covering newspaper flapped in the strong wind and a trail of ash, blown from her pan, followed her stout figure and swirled in the air to join the soot from the nearby factories and houses and settle on the proud, once clean, washings all around.

As she disappeared back into the close, Patchy again cast his eyes over all the windows, making sure that no one was watching, then he quickly ran out, pounced on the chosen garments, while noting with satisfaction that they were dry, hurried back into the close and changed in the open lavatory. Rolling his 'home gear' into a tight bundle, he tucked it behind the broad pipes at the back of the 'pan' and quickly took off back through the close and again into Rutherglen Road, where he hurried off towards the centre of the city.

He had often thought that if he ever did run away the last thing he would do would be to make for his own home, deciding that this would be the first place the police or the Brothers would search. But now as he took stock of his 'new' clothes, be realized how conspicuous the short trousers he was wearing would make him and decided that regardless of the danger he would have to pay his own house a visit.

Crossing the road into Richmond Park, Patchy decided to make his way through the park, over the bridge, into Glasgow Green and so to Bridgeton and Dalmarnock, but as the patch opened to reveal the deserted grass beyond, he recognised the danger of a lone, easily spotted figure crossing the empty park.

On a summer day, the huge park would have been a hive of activity. Lying on the south side of the Clyde it was a haven of grass, flowers and trees where the working-class of Gorbals and Hutchesontown could escape from the dark sooty tenements around and spend a few hours or even a 'day out', sitting on the grass or benches, eating sandwiches and drinking tea from flasks. The lucky ones could be seen queuing for 'pokes' from the occasional Italian, who having escaped internment, could still be found in the streets and parks of Glasgow selling ice cream from the huge coloured boxes which adorned the front of their bicycles. The pond inside the park was a favourite attraction for thousands of children from even as far away as Rutherglen and Cambuslang, who hung over the sides or even paddled about in the dirty water, catching 'baggy minnies' or sailing boats. A little beyond the pond, the swans could be fed or annoyed according to the outlook of the individual child and the resources available to him.

Young mothers with babies in prams or shawls, sat on the benches or on the grass and knitted and sewed and gossiped. Out from the centre of the park, under the trees and on the grass at the side of the river, stretched the 'unfortunates'. Without even the price of a bed in one of the many model lodging houses in the surrounding areas, the down-and-outs, both male and female, spent their days in the park catching up on their sleep. They were a familiar sight and even in inclement weather could be found on the park benches covered with newspapers to keep out the cold.

But on this bleak winter's day Patchy could see only four people in the park and decided that a fifth, particularly a big, guilty looking boy in short trousers would be just the thing to attract attention. He turned and made his way back down the path and out towards Shawfield and so to Main Street Bridgeton where he mingled with the Saturday shoppers. Taking a short cut across to Dalmarnock, he turned into Franklin Street and immediately cursed himself for not having stuck to the main road.

Any other time he would joyfully have welcomed the attentions of the dozen girls who now waylaid him; pushing and pulling each other in order to kiss and hug him, but today Patchy's mind was far from romance. But, even in his agitated state, he was unable to suppress a smile as, still clutched by two of the girls, he viewed the scene before him. Having just finished their work at a box factory two streets away, the girls were the traditional escort for one of their number, soon to 'take the plunge'. The bride-to-be was jammed inside a high pram. Her face was covered in a mixture of soot and lipstick and on her head was a gent's bowler hat, which served as a head dress for her veil of ragged curtain material. Her top half had been stuffed at the front so that she strained over a fifty-odd inch bust and pinned on her coat were streamers and old bits of cloth. On her feet, which were sticking over the end of the pram, was a pair of men's working boots and clutched on her lap was the fertility charm — a white enamel 'chanty' packed tight with salt, on top of which sat a tiny cellulose doll. While two of the girls still clung to Patchy, the remainder dragged the 'bride' from the pram and placing the 'chanty' on the ground, they ran on either side of her calling 'hard up,' and 'I'll get ye,' as she was made to jump three times over the pot. Then they dragged the screaming girl over to Patchy and made her kiss him to which the boy responded as gallantly as he could. As 'bride' and 'chanty' were again bundled into the pram and the procession moved off, Patchy moaned in despair and tried to wrestle free of the girls holding him, to no avail. Grasping the luckless boy, the singing, laughing, shouting girls made their way round to Main Street, Patchy in their midst and danced and jigged their way towards the Cross. Spotting a crowd of boys gathered round a well-known, if still hopefully unobtrusive 'bookie', the girls screamed their way towards this new 'talent' and Patchy seizing his opportunity, freed himself and ran through the 'bookie's close', into Megan Street and out on the Dalmarnock Road.

The 'check' key was in the door of the third storey room and kitchen and he quickly turned it and entered to find to his relief that the house was empty.

Wasting no time, he foraged through drawers, cupboards and wardrobes till he found an old suit and a pair of brown brogues belonging to his brother Jimmy and these he quickly donned.

Taking care to leave the house as he had found it, he took a pound note from a tumbler on the mantelshelf and parcelled up his 'housey' boots and trousers, intending to discard them in the 'midden'.

He had closed the door behind him and quietly made his way to the first landing before he heard a voice in the close which he recognised as that of Brother Gabriel.

The Prefect on realizing that Patchy had flown, had quickly organized a search party consisting of McAleer, the farmer, Tommy the gardener and three of the most trusted boys, in order to scour the grounds. When this proved fruitless, he had first alerted the police, and then, after requesting Leon's permission to use his old Ford, had continued his search in the lanes and streets surrounding the school, stopping every so often to enquire from passers-by whether they had seen a boy of Patchy's description. Having armed himself with the boy's address, he had then made straight for Patchy's home and was now questioning Mrs McFarlane downstairs as to the whereabouts of the Kellys.

Not waiting to hear the conversation below him, Patchy quickly opened the landing window, deposited his bundle on the ledge of the lavatory window which ran alongside, then skilfully made his way down the rusty roan pipe to the backcourt.

Running through familiar closes and railings, over broken dykes and across roads, he finally arrived at Glasgow Cross.

A cup of tea and two hot pies in the National Restaurant in the Gallowgate at sevenpence, now left Patchy with nine and five in his pocket.

If only he could get down to England, he thought, but eight and ten wouldn't even take him to the border, never mind London or Southampton. Jimmy, his elder brother had joined the Merchant Navy, but he, Patchy couldn't go and enlist in Glasgow, he would need to go South, but how?

Savouring the grease on his lips from the mutton pies, he made his way along the Trongate which was crowded with Saturday shoppers, happily rejoicing in his illegal freedom. He walked through Woolworth's and Mark's and the Poly, but did not see an opportunity to purloin anything worth the kind of money he was looking for.

Pleased to see that no one was looking at him suspiciously, he felt once more like a normal human being, and even managed a cheeky wink at a couple of good-looking shop girls.

His stolen blue woollen jersey was warm against the dry but cold December weather and the chatter of the shopping crowds, intermingled with the clip-clop of horseshoes on the cobbles and the clanging of the trams made him feel secure and unhaunted.

His quest for money still strong, Patchy was taking

a special interest in the small jewellers' shops dotted the length of Argyle Street. As he wandered round to Buchanan Street, which sheltered some of the 'toffiest' shops in Glasgow, his attention was drawn to the jewellers shop whose large doorway ran at an angle from Buchanan Street into the Arcade. The window on either side of the doorway contained a twinkling selection of watches, necklaces, bracelets and every other kind of trinket, but mostly engagement rings. There was a fair-sized crowd peering through the glass, largely made up of servicemen and their girls, no doubt picking their ring for Christmas engagements. Every so often a young girl would emerge from the throngs, dragging behind her a reluctant serviceman to peer and point and coax at the window. Patchy noticed with satisfaction that the interior of the shop was also packed. All the salesgirls were busy and most important of all, there was a couple of twelve-year-old boys casually looking around who were certainly suspicious looking and were, no doubt much to their annoyance, the subject of any spare attention which the salesgirls might have. He waited until he saw two women, looking like mother and daughter, enter while gazing around. These Patchy followed, as if he were one of the party. Luck was certainly with him today and he was scarcely inside the door when he spotted a tray of watches lying at the corner of two glass counters. The nearby harassed assistant had just brought forward a second selection for a fur-coated customer, and didn't look sideways as Patchy, quick as a flash, slid the tray from the counter and under his blue jersey.

Inconspicuous in the crowds, he hurried to the Central Station and made for the lavatories. Here, in the privacy of a cubicle, he took the seven watches from the board and placed them in his pockets. They all looked beauties. Patchy who had never possessed a watch had difficulty in evaluating them, but they certainly looked good and with any luck would give him the fare to Southampton and more.

After tearing the board into tiny pieces, which he flushed away, he re-emerged from the smelly toilets where strange-looking and sexually-orientated men were milling around.

In the station itself, a hard knot of people had separated themselves from the hundreds moving to and fro and had gathered outside Platform 13. Moving towards them and peering over the shoulders of a small woman he saw a long line of German soldiers, obviously in transit from one prisoner-of-war camp to another.

The Germans looked dejected and forlorn, while the crowds seemed pleased to see them. Patchy watched with great interest this tiny part of the great drama of World War Two which was being played out before him. Here were Britain's enemies, caught and disarmed and now prisoners, far from home. Patchy felt a sneaking sympathy for them, yet at the same time thrilled even more at the realization of his own freedom.

These ordinary-looking men could be prisoners for years and years. God, fancy being a prisoner with Gabriel for years and getting beaten! Did prisoners get beaten, he wondered? Didn't remember hearing anything about that. Ah! well, hard cheese if they did!

Unaware that he had just missed Patchy in the close, Gabriel had first toured the streets of Dalmarnock and then, knowing that railways stations were gravitational forces for the lonely and the haunted, and that on three previous occasions absconders had been found in them, made his way, first to St. Enoch's and now to Central, where he peered over the heads of the crowds. Unable to resist a curious look at the Germans, he had stood watching for a few moments, all the while keeping a wary eye open for the missing boy.

But for all his zeal and perceptiveness, he did not see Patchy, though the boy at once spotted him. Quickly he went down the station stairs into Union Street and walking briskly towards the Grand Central Picture House, he paid his sixpence and sank comfortably into a back seat, enjoying the darkness and the heat and in no time he was fast asleep.

'Come, come I want you only,' sang McKeown to his pal Quigg.

'Ach, don't be daft, they'll think you're a bum boy,' laughed Quigg. 'Anyway, I didn't say I liked the picture, but it was better than staying in here on a Saturday afternoon. Here – did you see those aeroplanes in the news? Zoom, weesh, bang!' Quigg curved his arm in the air and zoomed down and up as he spoke. 'My brother's in the Air Force, maybe he was in one of those planes.'

'I'm going into the Navy,' chipped McKeown, 'you can go all over the world.'

102

'Aye, if the war's still on when we get out of this dump.'

'I'm going to see Gabriel tonight and see if I can't get out of here. I've never been in any bother and since my da' died, my mother needs me to get a job.'

'Some hopes you'll have. When did anybody ever get out before their time?' replied the despondent Quigg.

'Well, then why do they see us on a Saturday night? You can ask them you know. I've heard that if you've got good behaviour, you sometimes get out early.'

'Aye, that'll be right.'

'Maybe, we could run away like Kelly. Wonder if they've caught him yet?'

The Saturday film had been something of a disappointment to the boys and they had found no means of imaginative escape in the musical escapades of 'The Chocolate Soldier'.

The outside world of war, with its attendant horrors, held no terror, and how delighted the boys would have been with a realistic film, complete with bombs, guns and killings where they could dream themselves each the Hero at the Front, calmly walking through a hail of bullets, bombs and grenades, to emerge unharmed from a sea of fire and kill off millions of Jerries.'

The news and the cartoon had slightly boosted their morale, but on a Saturday night, spirits were always at a low ebb. After an afternoon of comparative freedom, even to a lousy picture, the boys always felt more claustrophobic and disgruntled on their return to the 'Marty'. The lucky ones would be home for the day on the morrow, but for those who had not yet served their seven months, there was no such light on

103

the immediate horizon to relieve the boredom of their term in the Approved School.

Astutely aware from his experiences in other schools that this was the peak period for brooding frustrations, Brother Alphonsus on taking up his appointment at Saint Martin's had introduced a 'Saturday interview hour' which served the necessary purpose of acting as a safety valve for the explosive yearnings of his charges.

'I came to see about getting out for good Brother.'

'Yes. Well, let's see now. Yes, you have been behaving yourself. You're in here sixteen months now. Yes, come back and see me in six weeks time.'

The sentence to Saint Martin's was always for an indefinite period, the indefinite period always being eighteen months, but the inmates never gave up hope and there was always somebody who knew somebody, who said that somebody had got three months remission for good behaviour.

The optimists never despaired and during their time at the school would pass on their belief to newcomers. The sceptics dismissed the possibility of remission as a rumour put about by the staff in order to maintain discipline.

But remission or not, there was always a queue of boys anxious to have a word with the Brother on duty at interview hour.

Tonight should have been Gabriel's turn, but as he was busily engaged in searching for Patchy, Brother Leon was now sitting at the table conducting the interviews.

Before him stretched a line of dejected unhappy boys, all with one thought in mind – when will I be out for good?

Curled up in the dark warmth of the cinema, Patchy dreamed of another world where he was plucking large, juicy, red berries from a line of bushes and eating one for every three he threw into the small bucket strapped to his chest. Moving from one bush to the next his steps became a slow motion dance where he was levitated more and more with every step he took, towards a clear fast flowing river. Rhythmically he began to circle in the air longer and longer, his action that of an ever increasing ripple which took him partway over the river and back and then halfway across again.

People swimming in the stream stopped and stood waist-deep in the water, gasping in wonder at his magical bouyancy, which was now taking him nearer and nearer the flower-decked bank and now to the bank itself, where he came down with a certain ecstacy which turned suddenly, in his moment of landing, to an eerie, creepy sensation.

This weird feeling he found to be justified when on awakening he found a fat curly-headed man half-leaning over him with his hand inside his fly.

'Ya dirty bastard,' Patchy yelled as the man rushed from the hall dragging a greasy raincoat, which he had been using the shield his 'amorous advances' from passers by.

'The dirty bastard,' muttered Patchy with a tremble, feeling in his pocket for the watches, which fortunately were all safely accounted for.

Consulting the cinema clock, he decided that as it was ten past eight, it was time he went about the task of finding a sleeping place for the night.

Outside it was dark and cold with a snowstorm blowing and figures stumbling hither and thither with torches. Patchy too stumbled through the streets away from the direction of the station, while pulling his lapels to his neck in an effort to trap the warmth and keep out the cold. On and on he went in an easterly direction, till he reached Bridgeton Cross, where he entered the billiard hall, just past the Cross.

A cousin of his worked there and Patchy hoped that with any luck, Jimmy Dunbar would help him to sell his watches and also get him a bed for the night.

But if Patchy expected to be welcomed with open arms, then a shock awaited him.

'My advice is for you to get back and give yourself up,' admonished Jimmy, passing a bottle of lemonade to his young cousin. 'Christ, you had only another three months to do and you'd have been out, wouldn't you?'

'Ah well, I've run away now, and I was wondering if you could put me up for the night,' said Patchy sticking a straw into the bottle, as he paid for it.

'I'll put you up for the night but that's all. God, look at you. You're frozen. You know it's only a single end I've got though, and there's not room to swing a kitten. You'll need to sleep on the floor and if you're wise you'll get up and give yourself up first thing in the morning. You get back and finish your time and don't be so bloody daft. You can sit over there just now till I get on with my work and I'll take you home later – but only for the night, remember!'

It was clear from Jimmy Dunbar's attitude that he would give Patchy little help, and the boy thought it wiser to say nothing about the watches. Despite the set-back however, he decided he would go it alone and settling himself on the steam pipes, he scanned the hall feeling that somewhere amongst the throng he would surely recognize a face that he could trust and who would help him. But the customer found Patchy before Patchy found the customer. A stocky man of average height, having finished his game and taking a break for a smoke, settled himself beside the boy on the pipes.

Colin Mack was a tough man and looked it. He had a small scar on his right cheek and a jutting chin which would have been frightening had it not lain beneath a constantly smiling mouth and dancing eyes which took in everything around him with scepticism, but also with a hint of merriment. He had spotted Patchy the moment the boy entered the hall.

'I haven't seen you in here before.'

'I haven't been here before; I'm looking for somebody to buy some watches,' said Patchy with little regard for the possible consequences. Fortunately his instinct had been correct.

'How much?'

'Ten quid for seven of them.'

'Let's have a look,' said Colin and Patchy pulled one from his pocket for the other's examination.

'Hold on a minute.' With this Colin moved to the other end of the hall. Patchy watching closely to make sure that the other wasn't off with his watch, saw him approach a shabbily dressed man with horn-rimmed glasses and thinning hair. The two of them moved away from the table at which the shabby man had been playing and Patchy saw the watch being examined. Now Colin indicated that Patchy should join them.

'Are they all like this?' asked the shabby man. Patchy pulled the six watches from his pocket and passed them over.

'I'll give you five quid.'

'Five quid for seven watches!' protested Patchy. 'I need ten!'

'You'll no get any more for them,' said the shabby man passing the watches back to Patchy, but at the same time sure that Patchy would accept his offer. And the boy would have done so, had he not at that moment caught sight of Jimmy Dunbat watching him from a nearby table.

'Right, don't bother.' he said, quickly returning the watches to his pocket, as the shabby man moved off.

'Tell you what I'll do lad,' said Colin who had remained by Patchy's side. 'I'll meet you here, tomorrow at four o'clock and I think I'll be able to get a customer for you. By the way what's your name?'

'Tommy – Tommy Kelly.'

'Mine's Colin Mack. So I'll see you at four tomorrow,' and Colin now hurried off to catch the pubs before they closed.

Next morning Patchy emerged from the pend in London Road and turned up the sleeves of the overcoat which his cousin had given him. He had never had an overcoat before and he had always told himself that there was something cissy about the wearing of one; but with the sleeves turned up to make it a neater fit, he found a new comfort in it as he followed the direction of the crowds and headed towards the barrows.

The second-hand market, the only live part of the

City and possibly of the country on an otherwise dull and typically dreary Scottish Sunday, attracted crowds from as far away as Falkirk and Stirling, and Bellshill and Lanark, and as Christmas toys, dollies and prams, forts, bikes and skates appeared on the stalls, so the crowds had grown, all fighting for bargains which they would take home wrapped in sheets of newspaper to boast they had bought for five shillings cheaper than normal, at the Barrows.

Dotted amongst the wholly working-class shoppers, could be found a fair number of small brown Lascar seamen, who even in these days of war and itinerant servicemen, seemed to be the only foreigners who had ever discovered this hub of Glasgow. They were a familiar sight to the regulars and to the stall holders to whom they were known as 'johnnies' and who had grown accustomed to haggling and bargaining with them over clothes, or footwear, or wirelesses or sewing machines.

'How much this jersey?'

'Two shillings, Johnny.'

'No, no, too much, I give you one shilling.'

'Well, let's make it one and six then, Johnny.'

'One shilling only, not a penny more, one shilling . . .'

Roaring 'Hi Ho, the Hi-Li,' the loud-mouthed Londoner was having the desired effect on the crowd before him. And Patchy watched as fond parents, believing that it was in fact their very last opportunity to obtain a bat and ball, thrust up impatient hands or pushed their way to the front of the throng to make the necessary purchase.

At the side of the Lane, stood 'Black Sambo', selling his Magic Medicine. Business appeared to be slow for him and his crowd seemed to consist mainly of small children and awed strangers, amused at the sight of one so big and black. But Patchy had heard of cures that the man had performed and seriously wondered if there was any truth in the African's claim that 'My mixture is guaranteed to cure all skin ailments – liver complaints and rheumatism.'

Across Moncur Street at the corner of Kent Street, the boy passed the usual weekend crowd of immigrant Irishmen who had gathered to chat and joke with their fellow countrymen. They were easily recognizable by their 'bum ticklers' as the short jackets which they wore were called.

Dodging out of the way of two· small boys being chased by an irate stall-holder, Patchy wondered if it would be worth his while 'picking up' some razor blades or cheap jewellery himself. But he resisted the temptation, judging that he had better first be rid of the watches he had appropriated the previous day.

Caught up in this pre-festival spirit where everybody seemed to have money to spend, Patchy decided to splash out with the cash in his pocket, reckoning that he could be well-off, once he had seen Colin and had exchanged his watches, and to this end he headed in the direction of the 'seafood' shop. After walloping into two plates of well-vinegared mussels, he carried out a bag of whelks and a pin with which to dislodge the boiled and salted creatures as he continued his fascinating journey around the Barrows.

He found it an exciting experience just to meander round the stalls watching goods being bought and sold and the faces of those performing the transactions. His father had been a hawker and until the idea of going to sea had entered Patchy's head, being a hawker

110

himself had been the height of his ambition, and this was being nostalgically rekindled with every fruit stall he passed.

Under the watchful eye of the Jewish owner, Patchy admired the Catholic half of a religious stall. Hung high on opposing sides of the stall were cheap framed prints of King Billy on his horse facing Pius XII and George VI looking towards the Blessed Virgin. Jesus with the Crown of Thorns was prominently displayed and lower down, hanging from string which stretched from one side to the other were an assortment of rosary beads and masonic insignias: Decorating the counter with a huge selection of gaily coloured cardboard crypts complete with tiny cut-out figures of Virgin, Child, Ass and Donkey, which the broad-minded hawker had given pride of place as it was approaching Christmas.

Patchy's stroll around the Barrows would have continued until a quarter to four as he had planned, but for the development of a commotion at a nearby ornament stall. An elderly housewife having discovered that her bag was open and her purse missing, had informed the stall holder who had sent a small boy for the police and Patchy spotting the appearance of the two uniformed men, moved off with an outward casualness which he did not feel.

Finding himself again in Kent Street and still the happy owner of a couple of bob, he made his way in the direction of London Road, towards Peter Rossi's famous ice cream shop. Patchy could remember having seen queues at only two shops prior to the war, one of these was Reid's Pie Shop and the other Peter Rossi's. Such was the fame of the delicious ice cream that people would make a special journey just to taste

111

it and at the weekends in particular, the queue would extend well into London Road. Nearing the corner where the shop had been, he found that all that remained of the premises and the three-storey building above was an empty space. Sadly he moved off recalling now that he had heard that the corner tenement had received a direct hit on the night Clydebank was bombed.

Wandering along Argyle Street, which in sharp contrast to his visit of the previous day, was now curtained in Sunday silence, Patchy's interest was drawn to a handful of men making their way up Brunswick Street. As he followed them up the narrow part of it, he was taken aback to find the street widen and reveal the sudden sight of hundreds and hundreds of listeners.

Patchy's religious teaching had not been neglected, but a religious argument was new to him and his only experience of politics was a hazy recollection of being carried on his father's shoulders on May Day with hundreds of men and women following Jimmy Maxton, walking and carrying red banners and singing songs. He could also recall how his mother had told him that John McLean had been put in jail for the workers and that if there had been a modern Jesus Christ, then he must surely have been John McLean.

'God is watching you – and you – and you,' said a tall, thin, well-dressed Minister, as he pointed and jabbed his index finger at his grinning listeners. 'HIS view can be likened to a huge cinema screen – divided into thousands of millions of tiny screens – and on each of these tiny little screens is a picture of – you – and you – and you!' The preacher was now warming to his favourite thesis. 'And not a sparrow . . .'

'That means we're all film stars,' roared back a little man, stubbing out the remains of his Woodbine.

'. . . And not a sparrow falls but he knows of it,' continued the tall man, choosing to ignore the remark and the laughter which had followed. 'and he is recording in the Golden Book the good deeds and in the Black Book the evil deeds . . . twenty four hours a day, seven days a week, while he is watching you — and you — and him there!'

'And what about you?' queried the little man.

'Yes, he is watching me too . . . and you . . .'

'He must get hellava bored watching me.'

'. . . How did they get their wealth?' a red-haired man with a tobacco-stained rasping voice was asking his hearers in an adjoining crowd. The Duke of Hamilton caught a poacher and the Duke says "This is my land" and the poacher says "How did you get it?" and the Duke says "My ancestors fought for it" and the poacher says "Well you can get off that horse and I'll fight you for it." ' Some of his listeners laughed but Patchy couldn't see the joke nor could he see the point when the orator proceeded to claim that the King was a Jew because of some wrong side of the blanket business which he claimed had taken place around 1222.

Another speaker reminded Patchy of the broken crucifix back at the Marty. 'All these Christians,' he said, 'are walking about with crosses around their necks because crucifixion was the mode of execution at the time of Christ. If Jesus had waited two thousand years and came down to America, and the Americans had done him in' (which according to the speaker they certainly would have) 'then his followers would be wearing wee electric chairs around their necks!'

113

In a corner of the Street, Patchy listened as a small, stooped, one-eyed man with only another two giggling boys for his audience, explained in a heavy lisping voice that 'Bob McLone was not really a German spy' and that 'They had no right to throw him out of his job in the Rolls Royce as a security risk; Bob McLone was never a German spy' he shouted over and over again, swinging his fist in the air.

Patchy, not caring much whether or not the little man was a German spy, left Brunswick Street wondering if the whole world had gone off its head, or what the hell it was all about. Anyway he had to meet Colin.

'What in the name of Christ are you doing here?' spluttered Jimmy Dunbar as he spotted Patchy peeping round the door of the Billiard Hall looking for Colin. 'You're mother's heart must be broken,' he continued without waiting for a reply. 'You promised me this morning that you would go and give yourself up.'

'I know, I know,' muttered Patchy, shamefacedly lowering his eyes, unable to look his cousin in the face, 'but I've got a wee bit business to do first.'

'Getting yourself into more bloody trouble are you? Ach, well, thank God you're not my problem,' said Jimmy turning on his heel.

Patchy greeted with relief the appearance of the smiling Colin.

'Hold on a minute,' said Colin, 'till I nip inside and see if my mate's arrived.'

'O.K.,' said Patchy, 'I'll wait for you here.'

Some minutes later Colin returned with the news that he was unable to find his friend. 'I wonder if he's gone out to Bothwell. Aye, that's probably where he'll be. Anyway even if he's not there, there's one or two other lads who'll probably be there that I can put you on to.'

Patchy had often heard of the Bothwell Hotel, which, being some eight miles from the City, complied with the Scottish licensing laws which said that only bona fide travellers might quench their thirst on the Sabbath. Despite the fact that the Scots had always lived with this law, come a Sunday, their desperation was no less than that of an American alcoholic at the introduction of Prohibition. As few Glasgow working men had motor cars with which they might conveniently comply with the travel requirements, they provided a source of revenue for the owners of the 'shebeens' places where the desperate could satisfy their liquid needs with a variety of refreshments. Unfortunately, too, a variety of liquids was usually cunningly mixed in the one drink, the grateful proprietor welcoming the opportunity to be rid of that which, when there was a choice, would be discerningly rejected. The bad booze, plus the alert Glasgow City Constabulary, frequently tipped off by a disgruntled customer did much to chase the population from the illegal taverns and outside the Boundary to such places as the Bothwell Hotel. Here, despite the increased Sunday prices, the drinkers could relax and enjoy their refreshment in the company of others who shared their predicament and bemoan the fate that had had them born North of the Border.

'Right lad,' said Colin, 'let's get on our way.'

The top deck of the bus was empty save for a middle-aged couple who had obviously spent a day at the Barrows and were surrounded with a variety of goods, mostly unwrapped, which they were endeavouring to stuff into a large shopping bag and cover with newspaper.

'Two halves to Blantyre, darlin',' said Colin, as the plump, hard-looking conductress approached.

'Two halves! Aye that'll be right — two to Blantyre,' she said punching hard at her shiny machine. 'My, but your grandfather's an awful comic,' she returned, addressing herself to Patchy. Patchy, embarrassed for Colin, tried not to smile, but the older man remained nonchalant.

'Now, now, you know what they say; the older they are the harder they fall,' said Colin, still unoffended. 'Here, when do you stop darlin?' he continued.

'Ach, I'm on till eight and I'm beat, I've done a double shift the day — I started at eight this morning,' replied the girl, glad to have somebody to talk to, and a match for Colin's banter.

'Ah ha, so your shift will be up at eight, very nice,' quipped Colin nudging Patchy while deliberately eyeing the girl all over.

'Aye, it jist might be,' said the conductress, 'but it'll no be ony concern of yours.'

'Seriously darlin,' we're going over to the Bothwell Hotel and we'd be glad to see you there,' pattered Colin.

'Ony other time I might take you up on that, but I clock out at Hamilton and I've an early rise tomorrow.'

'Ah, too bad sweetheart, and are you hard to get up in the morning?'

'Aw, give over,' said the girl, moving away to chase back downstairs two small boys who had just alighted. 'Right inside you,' she roared, taken aback as she spotted their father behind them. 'Aw, I thought they were jist themselves,' she explained allowing them to pass.

'She was married,' said Patchy as Colin leaned over him to peer out of the window to see where they were.

'Aye, I know,' said Colin. 'Her man's probably in the Army, anyway it was just a line o' patter, I wasn't serious. Two stops after this yin is ours,' he added as the bus drew to a halt.

'Cheerio, sweetheart, remember now, you know where to find us if you want a good time,' he roared to the conductress as they jumped off the bus.

'Aye, sure, cheerio,' the girl waved cheerily back at them.

'What if she comes to Bothwell,' said Patchy, wondering what would become of him should he be deserted by his friend in strange territory.

'No a chance,' said Colin, sure of himself. 'Here let's get a move on, before it gets any darker.'

They picked their way over a rough road and in the fading light Patchy could just make out the outline of a bridge.

'Here's Bothwell Bridge now,' said Colin, 'and that there,' pointing to a white house just beyond the bridge 'is David Livingstone's Cottage.' 'Right won't be long now,' he continued as they moved over the rushing water, 'just over here and then we're in Bothwell.'

Colin was fairly stepping it out and Patchy only just managed to keep abreast of the older man. Now walking between the 'bought' houses with their neat gardens and trees, Patchy was enjoying the long denied exercise of a brisk evening walk.

'What's that?' he asked suddenly gripping Colin's sleeve, as coming from the opposite direction there marched a little band of about ten girls all dressed in brown and accompanied by three figures with long black robes and white bibs, which, at first glance, Patchy had guiltily mistaken for Marist Brothers.

'Ah, poor wee boy, did the nuns scare you?' said Colin sarcastically, at the same time eyeing the passing girls. 'They're frae the Convent there,' he said pointing back at a wall over the top of which hung high winter bare trees.

'Are they orphans?' enquired Patchy taking in the good brown 'dexters' and school hats and yellow brown and blue scarves in which the girls were wrapped.

'Naw, naw, it's a school, but I think some of them stay there all the time.' replied Colin, having lost interest in the unattainable females and anxious to be out of the cold.

As they neared the Hotel, Patchy felt young and awkward at the idea of entering such a 'lush' establishment, but soon relaxed in the atmosphere of the bar which was filled with a mixture of servicemen and familiar working-class types.

The barman looked twice at Patchy as Colin ordered the beer.

'You're a bit young son, are you not?'

'Not at all, he's a nephew of mine,' said Colin pompously, an answer which strangely enough appeared to satisfy the barman who pulled and placed before them the two foaming pints.

118

Patchy felt a warmth for Colin whose company he was enjoying and who was giving him so much assistance in the sale of his watches, and was now treating him like a man and buying him drink.

'Tommy Kelly,' mused Colin, as they sat down at a small round table, 'A took ye right away for a Protestant when I saw yer jersey, but it's no much like a Protestant name.'

Patchy taken aback, but seeing the danger of losing his only friend, replied apologetically 'I'm no' a Protestant . . . I'm a Catholic.'

It was now Colin's turn to be surprised. 'Funny, I can usually tell, and I could have sworn you were one of us.'

Patchy shook his head, 'Naw, I'm a Celtic Supporter, I suppose it must have been the jersey,' he said tugging at the now offensive woollen, while flickering a small hopeful smile at the other, 'but my cousin – the one that works at the Billiard Hall – he's a Protestant . . .'

This final statement seemed to decide Colin and much to Patchy's relief, the older man gave him a friendly nudge. 'Ach well, I suppose it takes all kinds to make a world! Here, just a minute, there's just the very man to help us,' he said pointing in the direction of the 'Gents' from which a tall handsome sandy-haired man with a huge 'crombie' overcoat had just swaggered.

Colin jumped up and headed in the direction of his acquaintance who after a few whispered words returned with him to Patchy.

'Let him see the watches, Tommy,' instructed Colin, sliding a hand over the top of the small table at which they were seated. Patchy slipped two from his pocket

119

and passed them to Colin, who moved them off the table and into the big man's lap.

'How many?' clipped the stranger.

'Seven in all,' said Patchy.

'Give you a pound apiece,' said the tall man.

'Aye, aw' right,' said Patchy reluctantly bringing the remainder of the watches from his pocket.

'He was offered ten,' lied Colin hopefully, sensing his friend's disappointment, 'but we just missed the lad with the money at the Billiard Hall.'

'You don't say,' said the big man, disinterested. He pocketed the watches in the folds of his heavy coat, then groped round to his hip pocket and withdrew a rolled bundle of notes from which he counted. 'Seven,' he said pushing the money across the table at the same time rising, and moving off without another word as if Colin and Patchy didn't exist.

As Patchy folded the money Colin collected another two pints from the bar.

'That should be worth about thirty bob tae me' said the older man.

'Here you are,' said Patchy pushing over two notes, 'there's two pounds and thanks a million, you're a real pal.'

'Don't mention it son,' replied the beaming Colin, pocketing the money. 'It was a pleasure.'

Patchy had downed his first pint, more interested in the result of the conversation than in what he was drinking. He didn't much fancy beer, which he had tasted before, but didn't want to appear less than a man to his companion by refusing it.

As Colin pushed forward the second round, Patchy lifted the large mug to his lips and without stopping for a breath, forced down a third of the drink.

120

'Where did you get the watches?' enquired Colin.

'I just walked into a shop in the town and picked them off the counter.'

'Just like that?'

'Aye, just like that,' said Patchy smiling proudly.

'I couldn't do that,' said Colin, 'I'm too feart, but the next time you get anything like that, you just come back to your Uncle Colin.'

'Uncle Colin?'

'Aye, that's right, you can just call me Uncle Colin. You're fond of the beer, I see.'

'Aye, but this is the first time I've really been inside a pub.'

'Get away — are ye serious?'

'Aye, cross my heart,' Patchy made the sign of the cross on his chest.

'For God's sake,' said Colin, hastily covering the boy's hand with his own, 'don't let anybody here see you making a sign like that!'

'Oh, I'm sorry, Col... Uncle Colin, I forgot.' Patchy was contrite.

'Oh, skip it!' said Colin, 'but what I was going to say to you was, never get too fond of the beer, son — a couple of pints. Be like your Uncle Colin — keep the money and the energy for the women.'

'Women,' Patchy was startled.

'You know what they are, don't ye?'

'Aye... sure, but...'

'No buts about it son — the birds are the thing. See that two quid you gave me? Well that'll get me an all-nighter, with a smashin' young thing... fancy it?'

'Aye... but.'

'But... nothing! Ye're a big enough man for a woman.'

121

'Sure . . . sure . . . great,' said Patchy already feeling his trousers bulge.

'Right then, finish up the pint, and we'll be off. I'll get you a woman alright!'

Jimmy Quigley picked up another six sausages, threw them into the sizzling hot fat and with the efficiency of a well-trained coffee stall chef, proceeded to cut and sparingly butter the bread rolls, at the same time casting an experienced omniscient eye into the snowflakes falling about the stall.

There was a snug feeling about standing over the warm stove with the smell of hot-dogs and hot tea surrounding him; and this was emphasized and reinforced with every glance out into the darkness where the shadowy figures of the night were lurking around.

A couple of British soldiers spending an hour between trains, snatching a welcome refreshment at one of the few places where such could be obtained during .the night in the blacked-out city, caught his eye and he wondered if they might be potential customers for Susy and Flo who he expected any minute to return from the 'short time' he had arranged for them with the two Free French sailors.

There was talk in the papers about people profiteering from the war, and some slight condemnation of the practice from the same sources, but Jimmy Quigley knew that there were plenty of big bugs who had made their fortunes from the First World War and he was determined to make his from the Second; by any means that made themselves available.

A Territorial Army man for eight years, he had walked up and down Grace Street in Anderson with a great deal of pride in his uniform and a willingness to fight for his King and Country; but had suffered the shame of being discharged with a cardiac condition four days after war had been declared, causing him to be held up to great ridicule in and around the Anderson Cross Area, where he had grown up.

The opportunities in wartime Glasgow for a young man who had been declared medically unfit for military service and who was without scruples, were enormous, and Jimmy Quigley had discarded his scruples with his army uniform to pursue his black marketeering, poncing and fencing activities with immense energy.

Buying and selling ration coupons, identity cards and insurance books as well as touting, ensured that he was fully occupied during the night hours, while ostensibly employed as an assistant coffee-stall attendant.

Never one to waste time, most mornings found Jimmy Quigley mingling with the casuals gathered in Cheapside Street, where prospective employers came to hire men by the day for work in the stores. These stores had been set up by the Government throughout the city and housed such things as tinned food, flour and other necessities, awaiting in readiness for any emergency which might arise and here the fortunate amongst the casuals could find a day's work for eleven and eightpence.

But Jimmy wasn't here to hire or be hired. His interest lay in the insurance card which each man carried with him.

As was to be expected, the casuals were usually

desperately in need of cash and a less persuasive tongue than Jimmy's could have successfully negotiated the transfer of insurance cards for an easily earned thirty shillings. Jimmy liked to keep a good stock of these, and reselling them at a fiver a time to even more desperate men on the run from the forces was an easy matter.

Right now, however, he would be confining his salemanship to tea, for as he peered sideways from the stove, he noted the approach of a familiar figure, that of Detective John Gallacher and a mate whom Jimmy did not recognize.

'Anything ado' tonight?' asked Gallacher quietly, as he accepted one of the steaming hot cups of tea which Quigley pushed across the counter. 'Naw, it's very quiet, very quiet indeed,' replied Quigley, joining the two policemen with a large mug of his own.

'Been selling any good ration books lately?' asked Gallacher, poker-faced.

'Come off it, come off it, you know I don't do anything like that.'

'Naw, I know you don't,' said Gallacher at the same time pushing a snapshot across the counter, 'Do you know that face?'

Quigley looked around him before answering, then lifting a dishtowel to wipe the counter, muttered 'Sure, that's Granger from the Cowcaddens; on the run is he?'

Quigley knew that Gallacher's speciality of the moment lay in capturing deserters, and as the policeman had on more than one occasion rescued him from the pitfalls of his poncing and fencing activities, he suspected that in Gallacher's eyes, desertion was the number one crime, and the one which he pursued hardest.

'Ye haven't seen him around, have ye?' said the policeman, ignoring the question.

'Naw, never, but the minute I do I'll give you the wire. Fancy a hot-dog?'

'Naw, I'll no bother — here have a look at this one.' Gallacher now pushed forward the picture of a younger man, a picture of Patchy Kelly, which Quigley studied for a moment.

'Cannae say I know him,' but if I see him I'll let you know right away.'

'You do that Jimmy.' Gallacher took a last sip of his tea beckoned his mate and together they moved off into the dark hub of the city in the direction of the Central Station Bridge.

Here servicemen, taking time off from their patriotic chores on behalf of America, Britain, Free France and Poland, swarmed and could often be seen in silent, lustful queues of anything up to a dozen, before equally lustful women of various ages, heights and colouring, who, with the start of the war, had suddenly emerged from God knows where.

Not infrequently, Quigley at his stall, had heard the night's silence erupt in a cosmopolitan babble of tongues, as perhaps a particularly impatient client would jump the queue, or a less impatient one object at the sight of his opposite number when his turn did finally arrive.

However, thought Quigley amused, these sights wouldn't disturb Gallacher. His eyes would be strained for his pet hate, deserters, the cornering of whom, it was said, had already won him rapid promotion from pounding a beat.

It appeared that Gallacher's activities were now mainly centered in the Gallowgate, where, if there was any truth in the current joke that should there be a German invasion, the Gallowgate would have to be declared an 'open city', the policeman would not find time heavy on his hands.

In fact Gallacher's enthusiasm in this direction was something of a legend and Quigley had just, the day before, heard a story, the truth of which he doubted as he himself would not underestimate Gallacher's intelligence, but it was said nevertheless, that Mad Meikle, now apparently discharged for reasons not unconnected with his nickname, had set things up for Gallacher. Making sure that the big policeman had spotted him and was in hot pursuit, he had taken off up the Gallowgate, down Watson Street, round Bell Street, and to Glasgow Cross where Gallacher had finally felled him in a rugby tackle only to become the laughing stock of those assembled at the Mercat Monument, as Mad Meikle produced his discharge papers, danced round all the old men and women there assembled, round all the children out for messages and the city commuters at the surrounding bus and tram stops, and invited their inspection, all the while laughing and pointing at the nonplussed policemen, before finally jigging his way back to Gallacher and ceremoniously presenting the Discharge Book to him.

Despite his silent amusement, Quigley found Gallacher a handy man to know, but his musings stopped as he had to return to work. As business picked up he turned his attention to the coffee-stall again, to the soldiers, insomniacs, petty thieves, modeilers and 'brass nails' and their customers, as they emerged from the dark slushy streets to order tea and dogs before retiring to the shadowy corners around the stall, to warm their tongues and their hands on the tea and

126

watch with varying degrees of interest, the other familiar and unfamiliar figures around.

Quigley knew most of the regulars and their motives as he also knew Colin and was no less aware of his motive, as he now approached in the company of a younger lad who Quigley thought looked vaguely familiar.

'A couple of dogs and two teas, Jimmy,' said Colin at the same time casting lecherous eyes over the ten or so women whose outlines could just be seen in the dim light allowed to flow from the stall.

'Two teas and two dogs.' Quigley accepted the florin and smartly passed the two copper coins in change.

'How's it goin' Colin?'

'Champion, champion,' replied the Bridgeton man, reluctantly dragging his eyes from the surrounding females. 'You missed a wee chance of some watches the day,' he said, now making short work of one of the hot dogs.

'Big deal, telling me now about bargains I've missed,' said Quigley, adding in a lower tone, 'who was selling them?'

'My young nephew here,' Colin indicated Patchy who now, while experiencing the effects of his first forbidden pints, and anticipating the unknown delights of his first woman, was feeling even more proud than he had earlier whilst actually engaged in the disposal of the merchandise.

'I've an awful notion I've seen you before,' said Quigley. 'What's your name?'

'Kelly, Tommy Kelly.'

'Tommy Kelly, where are you frae?'

'Dalmarnock,' replied Patchy, copying Colin's manner of nonchalantly answering the coffee-stall man while eyeing the women at the same time.

'We're looking for a couple of bits of crumpet,' said Colin, querulously eyeing Quigley while the latter rubbed his greasy hands on an even more greasy and less than white apron. 'Anything decent about?'

'What's up with them that's there?' Quigley unobtrusively moved a finger and eye in an encircling movement that took in every female within sight of the stall. 'I didnae know you were that particular.'

'I just don't like eating the same cabbage twice.' Colin, unabashed, winked at Patchy, who gave a smiling flicker of the eye in return.

'There'll be a couple here later; I'll put you on to,' said Quigley, turning away to serve a small Gordon Highlander who was now laying his large kitbag down in the slush.

Patchy's blood flowed pleasantly fast as he secretly measured himself against Colin and found that he had an advantage of fully three inches over the older man, who between sips of the hot tea, was now giving his experienced assessments of the females around.

'That's Aberdeen Jean there,' he whispered, indicating a tall red-faced woman with haggard blue eyes who was now busily engaged in conversation with the Gordon Highlander. 'She dosnae look much, but she's some bed worker. Do you fancy her?'

'Aye, no bad,' said Patchy reluctantly, trying to appear as expert as his companion and resolutely dismissing, even to himself, the fact that he had only once been with a female and that when he was twelve years old, when Mary Merrior of his own age invited him to do 'dirty things', in an outside toilet in Montieth Row. He had been rebuked on that occasion,

128

sullenly dismissed with 'You cannae dae it right, Kelly.'

'. . . No Bad,' he repeated, 'But here, I fancy that big black bird better,' he continued enthusiastically, as he caught sight of the beautiful, supple, dark-skinned girl who now approached the stall.

'Nice, isn't she?' Colin appeared nonchalant. 'I was with her last week, and there we were stripped naked in this empty house in the South Side, when this big polis burst in and shone his torch on us, and what do you think he said?'

'I don't know, what did he say?'

'Dr. Livingstone, I presume?'

'Aye, that'll be right,' said Patchy, at once appreciating the joke and giving his friend a quick nudge, 'But here, I wouldnae mind getting her in an empty house the night myself.'

While Patchy and Colin were thus engaged, the dark African beauty, known as Black Val, had been approached by a large, loose-jointed, heavy-jowelled American who appeared, even to Patchy's somewhat inebriated eye, to have had too much to drink.

'They've too much bloody money, these Yanks,' muttered Colin enviously, while turning away from the sight of the stuffed wallet which the American was now flashing at Black Val, who it seemed was a little hesitant about joining the soldier, 'and they put up the bloody prices.'

'Here, who's that one there?' Patchy pointed to a plump, attractive blonde who had just appeared and was now busily engaged in conversation with Quigley.

'I've never seen her before, but I'll find out.' Colin straining his ears, eased slightly forward in an endeavour to hear.

'Did it go alright?' he heard Quigley ask as he

pushed a cup of hot tea towards the blue-eyed girl he knew as English Mae.

'Yeah, fine, but I'm beat, I'm off to bed now Jimmy. See . . .'

'How about taking the lad there with you,' interrupted Quigley, indicating in the direction of Colin and Patchy.

English Mae, looked not displeasingly towards the two, and half-heartedly protested, 'But gees Jimmy love, I'm tired . . .'

'It's worth a couple of quid.' Quigley turned towards his sizzling sausages as the American who had been snubbed by Black Val now swayed towards the counter and put his gangling arms around English Mae.

'I like you, honey,' said the soldier, whose leering smile grew wider as the girl responded by putting her arms around his stout waist. He alone was unaware of the fact that English Mae's fingers were slipping into his hip pocket and extracting the wallet which he had been so keen on displaying to the other girl, who by now was walking off with one of the two young English soldiers.

'How say you and I go have a good time?' said the soldier, slackening his grip on the girl.

'I'm sorry,' Mae now moved off in the direction of Colin and Patchy, 'but I'm already with someone.'

Colin's eyes lighted with lustful hope as she approached, and then dimmed with disappointment as she passed him to stand close in front of Patchy. She proceeded to wind her arms around the boy's neck while pressing her full breasts against his pounding heart. 'Sure I am?' she murmured, drawing her hot lips teasingly across Patchy's and then disentangling her arms from his neck, she put her left arm possessively through the crook of his right elbow.

'You sure are,' agreed Patchy as he jauntily moved off into the night, the girl on his arm, completely unmindful of the abandoned Colin.

'You know, love, you look just like my kid brother,' said English Mae, 'you've got lovely brown eyes, just like his.'

'I like your eyes too,' said Patchy, delighting in the feel of her breast against his arm.

'Got two quid, have you?' English Mae moved her head closer as the boy fished in his pocket for the paper notes.

A dark silence permeated the city through which they now walked arm in arm.

To English Mae, Patchy was just another, if rather young client with whom she would go through the business. To Patchy she was a clean, wholesome and warm woman who was filling every inch of his body with a cosy, stimulating excitement he had never before known.

They had now reached Midland Street and in the additional darkness of the tunnel Mae leaned against the wall and pulled Patchy towards her, more moved by the thought of getting it over quickly and retiring alone to the comforts of her bed, than by the passion she now enacted.

Patchy, willingly pressed against her, to find that Mae had already loosened her coat and blouse, and as his hands joyously grasped and petted the large bare breasts, her cold fingers expertly parted his fly to

131

bring forth his solid stalk of expanded muscle, now stretched to a length he had never known.

Patchy's own hand instinctively lowered to raise the girl's skirt and then grip both sides of her silk knickers, while Mae expertly wriggled her hips, further adding to Patchy's mounting excitement, but at the same time enabling him to lower the restricting underwear sufficiently to allow the manipulation of his pulsating manhood between her warm thighs, and up into the unknown, if not unexplored cavity. Immediately his body exploded in a premature rocket of delight, that sparked and stung and returned again and again, tingling every nerve in his already trembling body.

Simultaneously, from the depths of the dark tunnel reverberated a loud clear American voice on the steel rafters and bricks, 'You cocksucking bitch, you frigging whore, you've got my wallet, you thievin' bastard.'

Patchy returned to earth with a thud, scarcely aware of what was happening. He automatically withdrew, his fingers moving over the buttons of his fly as Mae made an endeavour to right her clothing, but not before the American, pushing Patchy aside, struck her a vicious punch across the face. 'You thieving whoring bastard, where's my wallet?' he demanded, one hand alternately shaking and slapping her while the other groped her clothing for the missing wallet.

The girl's screams tore through Patchy's ears, and with a fearlessness he had never before experienced, he fell upon the American, pulling his head towards him and butting him on the nose, bringing forth a stream of blood, which the soldier instinctively tried to stem with his hands.

132

As the American bent forward, Patchy gripped his hair tight in one hand and with the other punched again and again at his bleeding face, until finally releasing him, the soldier dropped to the ground and lay softly moaning.

'Come on,' he vaguely heard Mae say, 'Come on, let's get out of here quick.'

'Did he hurt ye, hen?' asked Patchy as they hurried towards Argyle Street.

'No, I'm alright, but don't call me hen.'

'I'm sorry, but what will I call ye?'

'Call me Mae — call me anything you bloody well like, but for Christ sakes, don't call me hen!' said Mae, no longer able to conceal the agitation she felt.

As they sat in the taxi, she seemed to relax a little. 'You know, you could have just run away, other men would have . . . they would be frightened to be caught with a woman on the game — what's your name anyway?'

'Tommy, Tommy Kelly.'

'Well Tommy, you can be my stick man,' and Mae moved closer putting her arm through his and for the first time really looking at the boy.

And she did indeed feel protected, and not at all like a brass nail or a lady of the street or a whore; and as she rested against the boy, she felt an affection that she could scarcely remember experiencing before.

At one in the morning Gabriel, after making a second search of the grounds of St Martin's, returned to his cold room. Two years before a runaway boy had lost his two feet to frostbite in an attempt to get away from the school in just such weather as this and Gabriel was perturbed that such a fate might also befall an unimaginative boy like Kelly. He was also beginning to fear that he himself might in some way be held responsible for the boy's absconding. Why had he absconded? Surely not because he had been about to cut his hair. No, surely not for that. Wouldn't it grow in again? And did he not deserve a haircut?

Kelly had been difficult right from the start, and nobody, thought Gabriel, could fault him for administering the necessary punishment. The boy had been wicked and the wicked had to be penalised. This was his philosophy. Yes, his actions had certainly been justified. But 'Spite' he had heard called out and this had indeed troubled him, but could he allow slumsters like these to dictate his ethics? Ridiculous, he thought, this class of boy, all from the same unimaginative background, had its own code, unknown and incomprehensible to others. Why should he allow them to disturb him, hadn't he always examined his actions? And had he ever once found them to be motivated by spite?

The school inspectors might ask some questions, but possibly if the boy was found this would be unnecessary. They, fortunately, realized the difficulty of this type of work, and hadn't they, on their last visit eighteen months before commended Gabriel for his discipline and obvious control over the boys?

Brother Gabriel, a little more contented, but still deeply troubled, knelt and prayed and asked the Lord that this wayward boy be found safe and well.

Seventy-three deserters Gallacher had returned to the colours. But never had he had the privilege of arresting an American AWOL. So he had been hoping that Top Sergeant Rakowski who had just stumbled into his arms with his complaint would prove to be the first, as he asked the angry drunken soldier for his papers.

But no, the American was on a fully authorized forty-eight hour furlough.

'You say you met her at the coffee-stall?' said Gallacher.

'Round that corner,' replied Rakowski, 'and that guy round there. He knew her.'

'Come on round with us,' said Gallacher's mate, handing Rakowski a handkerchief to replace the reddened rag he had been holding to his nose. 'Then we'll get you to the Infirmary.'

'It's O.K.' said Rakowski. 'It's stopped bleeding now. Hell, all I want is that wallet of mine back.'

'How much was in it?'

'Eighty dollars.'

Quigley was quick to give the required information. 'English Mae it was,' he stated bluntly as he washed a cloth and cleaned the counter.

'We'll soon lay hands on her,' said Gallacher.

'What's her address?' came from his burly mate, notebook and pencil in hand.

'London Road... near Kent Street,' Quigley coughed up. 'I don't know the number.'

'I know it,' said Gallacher, a walking computer on Glasgow's underworld. 'And who was the man she was with?'

'A young fella about eighteen,' said Quigley, 'said his name was Tommy Kelly. From Dalmarnock I think.'

'Thomas Kelly,' said Gallacher's mate, recognition dawning, as he nodded to Gallacher 'That wouldn't be . . .'

Gallacher already had the photograph out and was showing it to the American and Quigley.

'That's the bastard,' said the Top Sergeant.

'I knew I'd seen him before,' said Quigley 'That's him alright.'

'You're sure?' said Gallacher and both nodded.

'We'll pick her up and then get him,' said his mate.

The coal fire set in the big black range still boasted a few dying red embers as Patchy and Mae entered the 'single end' which Mae referred to as her flat.

Taking some sticks from a brass box at the corner of the fireplace she set to work rekindling the fire. Holding a newspaper against the black ribs, she waited till the few remaining red coals responded to the draught below, igniting the broken sticks to send them crackling and sparking into light. Snatching at the newspaper when it too threatened to burn she quickly rolled it into a ball, threw it into the now merry flames and topped the lot with some small pieces of coal.

Patchy sat on the large armchair watching.

Washing her hands and then extinguishing the main light in the centre of the ceiling, she clicked to life a small red lamp then moved over to sit on the arm of his chair. Taking the brown leather wallet which had once been the property of the American soldier, from a patch pocket on her skirt, she proceeded to examine the paper contents.

Patchy, disinterested, slipped an arm around her waist, and spread small kisses around the valley of her breasts, which exposed by the part open blouse, were now level with his face.

Pushing him gently from her, she put aside the wallet and kneeling before him guided his eager hands to her blouse. Opening the bottom button she left him to release those remaining and remove her upper garments while she herself disposed of the restricting skirt and knickers. His hands flicking and sliding down her body, she rose to stand wriggling before him in black suspender belt and silk stockings. Turning from him so that her buttocks were now before his face she unfastened the belt, felt for his hands and signified her intention by guiding them to the top of her hose and pushing downwards. Then she turned and stood close and warm and naked before him, sensuously rejoicing in his tremble as with dilated eyes, gentle hands and pursed lips he rose. She felt her nipples push from her breasts to scratch against the rough woollen jersey. He eased away to remove the stolen jersey and shirt and then trousers and vest, his eyes never leaving Mae as she turned and writhed and swung and swayed, her own dark eyes full of admiration and desire for his young strong supple body and prominent manhood. Then with breasts pushed forward and legs apart she invited him. And Patchy, love and tenderness filling his heart was enfolded in her eager frame while Mae the whore was extinguished and Mae the woman rejoiced in the full flow of this harsh invasion of her body.

The loud knocking of the door was unmistakably that of authority. Six quick raps, which reverberated throughout the entire building and rattled through Patchy's brain, punctured the rainbow dream balloon where Mae and he swirled in multicoloured mists of falling daisies, and recalled him to the hard and miserable realities of his young life; which seemed never to have had a beginning and to have no forseeable happy end.

He jumped from the bed and shook his slumbering partner.

'Mae! the police,' he whispered.

'Open up there,' Gallacher's voice boomed from the landing, reinforcing Patchy's whisper and bringing the sleeping girl from her bed.

'What do they want?' still half-asleep and befuddled, she was pulling on an underskirt.

'Right! Open up there, it's the police!'

Patchy pulling his braces over his shoulders took a few tip-toed steps to the window, lifted the blackout blind and gazed down into the street, three flights below.

'Have you got a warrant?' asked Mae from the inside of the door.

'Open up or we'll warrant this fuckin' door in,' came Gallacher's voice, which sentiment he emphasized with a strong bang on the door with his boot, causing it to shake on its rusty hinges.

'All right, all right,' said Mae, pulling down the 'snib' and turning the large locking key to open the

138

door, allowing the two burly policemen to enter.

'Right,' said Gallacher moving in the direction of the range as his eyes surveyed the room. His big hands swooped over the mantlepiece, moving in all directions, then the high chest of drawers, pushing aside jars and ornaments, and scattering kirby grips and curlers over the side to the floor. Moving to the small table, he immediately spotted the wallet. Picking it up he opened it and turned to Mae who was standing defiantly watching.

'Get your clothes on you, you're going down to the station with me, and you too, Son,' he said tossing the pullover from the couch to Patchy.

'What have we done – what are we being charged with,' said Mae in a last defiant attempt at evasion.

'This, this is what you've done!' said Gallacher, opening the wallet flat and holding it in front of her eyes.

Mae stared straight ahead as if she hadn't seen.

'And assault!' added Gallacher, turning in Patchy's direction and regarding the boy squarely but without excessive severity.

'But what . . .' began Patchy.

'Say nothing love,' interrupted Mae.

'Say nothing! Does this here no say plenty, hen?' Gallacher indicated the wallet in his hand from which he read: 'This is the property of John Rakowski, 1847N Maple Throng . . .'' Are you John Rakowski, Son,' he asked Patchy, 'Are you from 1847 Maple?'

'Say nothing,' Mae interrupted again, turning to the frightened boy and at the same time fastening the last button on her blouse before slipping on her high-heeled shoes. 'Say nothing!'

'You cannae be John Rakowski, son,' said Gal-

139

lacher's mate sarcastically, 'because you're Tommy Kelly and you're from Dalmarnock.'

'I'm saying nothing.' said Patchy, feeling that English Mae's advice came from some vast storehouse of experience and wisdom.

'Thomas B. Kelly,' repeated the policeman, 'alias Patchy, big-time absconder,' he added, bringing a start from the frightened youth.

As the policeman moved towards him, he revealed to Patchy a direct path leading to the door, towards which he instinctively ran, pushing a chair over on the policeman's legs.

In a second he had the door open and was running, stumbling and tripping down the three flights of stairs, crashing against the walls with the flats of his hands, smacking against the brown blistered paint, tumbling over in his haste and rising neatly and quickly, knowing somehow that he had enough of a start to get out of the close and away, far away he knew not where — from the arms of the law.

He heard Gallacher clumping down the stairs, but he ran and ran and stumbled and ran and stumbled until he reached the flat of the dark close at the bottom of the stairs and on and on, scarcely aware of the wet snow and slush beneath his feet, forgetting, and unable to see the protective baffle wall two feet from the end of the close. His feet slid from under him, throwing him forward, body and wall met, and Patchy's head cracked before he fell, blood spurting from his left ear.

It had taken Gallacher two full seconds to realize that the boy was making a run for it. Nearing the bottom of the stairs, he heard the hard thud as Patchy's head hit the baffle outside the close. Shining his torch, Gallacher picked out the figure lying on the wet slush. Seeing that the boy was injured, the big detective raised him in his arms before he realized that he was unconscious. Lifting him, he sensed that this was indeed a boy and not the hardened criminal that he was obviously attempting to be. Light enough for Gallacher to lift, the big policeman carried him half the length of the close to where it was dry before gently lowering him under the small flicker of gas-light which now fell upon Patchy's face.

Innocent he looked thought Gallacher, harmless and completely unconscious.

'You got him John?' his mate shouted from behind and Gallacher turned to see him pushing English Mae before him while keeping a tight grip on her twisted sleeve.

'What have you done to him — what have you done? You've killed him,' shouted Mae, gripping Gallacher's shoulder and trying to shake him about.

'All right, all right, take it easy... he's hurt himself, ran into the baffle.' With a wave of the hand he dismissed her as Patchy began to moan softly. 'Take her down to the station, Sam; we'll need to get an ambulance for this one.' Drawing his whistle from his pocket and rising he went to the front of the close and blew three loud, long shrill blasts. Then returning to the others, who still stood over Patchy. 'Get rid of her, Sam.' indicating Mae, who was now quietly weeping.

As English Mae and the policeman disappeared into the darkness, Gallacher took a big handkerchief from his pocket and held it against Patchy's ear. 'Silly wee boy...'

Hearing approaching footsteps, he softly blew his

whistle, and almost immediately a beat policeman appeared, one hand on his baton, the other on a torch.

'Are you all right?' said the constable unnecessarily.

'Call an ambulance, quick,' said Gallacher, watching Patchy's face as consciousness flickered over it. 'He's coming to now . . .' with which the constable took his leave.

'Are you O.K. son?'

'What happened?'

'You bashed your head on the baffle, take it easy now, don't try to move.'

Lying there, looking up into the flickering gas flame, cold stone beneath him and a policeman's hand on his shoulder; an awareness suddenly dawned on the boy. This he despaired, was the destiny for which he had been born. Life was hopeless, dark and dingy and held out no promise for him.

'. . . taking me back to Saint Martin's?'

'First of all we'll need to get you to the Infirmary and get you fixed up.'

'And then to the Marty?' said Patchy, turning his head slightly to ease the pain on the left side.

'Naw, I'm afraid not son, assault and robbery — that's a serious charge. You're for another chip shop now — one where they fry bigger fish!'

The sloping roof of Saint Martin's swooped sharply to canopy the main entrance situated at the left wing of the Approved School. The front door of heavy, thick, brown wood, encased in a black metal frame, which by night faced the outside world, was pulled back against the wall of the tiny inside hall, whose only other wall supported a large crucifix of the same dark brown colour as the door, and contrasted sharply against the cream paint of the walls and ceiling.

On the fourth side of the entrance lay another, less imposing door of glass, which now opened to reveal Gabriel, tall, handsome and clean, his red wavy hair with just a suggestion of the water which had recently been combed through it.

Gabriel stepped on the coloured marble floor and moved down the two steps to the gravel path to gaze down the long avenue of trees, at the foot of which the large gate, now open, revealed a suggestion of the streets and lanes of the suburb beyond.

Behind him, the school, if quiet, was none the less industrious.

In the Bakehouse, the 'baker boys' kneaded and mixed and baked; the 'cobbler boys' in their own little room, bent over their lasts, and hammered and sewed and brought nails to and from their mouths; the 'piggery boys' emptied troughs and journeyed to the kitchens and back with feed for their charges; the 'tailors' sewed and pulled and darned and patched; and out in the fields the 'farmers' trampled about in their heavy boots and prepared the soil for the spring planting; and the under fourteens in the classrooms were counting and spelling and singing 'Like a Golden Dream' and envying the 'all day workers'. And every one of them was dreaming of the day when he would be 'out for good.'

Ahead of him Gabriel now spotted that for which he had been waiting.

'Brother Gabriel,' Sister Tierney's voice interrupted

his thoughts and he turned to find her standing at the glass door which he had left ajar. 'I wanted to have a word with you, I thought you would be anxious to know . . .'

Gabriel moved up the two steps to face her in the small hall . . . 'Yes, Good morning, Sister Tierney.'

'Kelly has been found, he . . .'

'Ah, that's good news, very good indeed,' said Gabriel, 'I was afraid . . .'

'. . . he's in the Royal Infirmary . . .'

'The. Infirmary . . .' Gabriel turned visibly pale. 'Why, what's . . .'

'Oh, it's all right, nothing serious,' said the nurse, bringing the colour back to Gabriel's cheeks. 'He had a slight concussion.'

'Oh! Thank God, he's safe.'

'Yes, apparently he ran into a baffle wall . . . running away from the police . . . he is charged with assault and robbery.'

'I'm not at all surprised,' said Gabriel, slightly angry, and turning his attention to the car which was coming to a halt thirty yards up the path.

'I thought you'd want to know . . . I'll be off now.'

'Yes, yes, thank you sister, thank you.'

Gabriel watched and listened as three doors of the four-door saloon car opened and slammed, and six feet came crunch, crunch crunching up the pink granite gravel towards him.

Two of the feet were those of a probation officer, the second pair belonged to the uniformed police driver and the third and smallest pair were those of the newest 'Marty Boy', a frightened looking thirteen year old.

144

Gabriel scanned the slip of paper which was now handed to him:

NAME	Duncan John McNulty
ADDRESS	10 Suffolk Street, Glasgow S.E.
DATE OF BIRTH	10.2.28
CONVICTION	Housebreaking.
SENTENCE	Indefinite period!

145